TURPIN'S APPRENTICE

England, 1761. Charity Bell is the daughter of an inn keeper. Her two elder sisters are only interested in marrying well, whereas feisty Charity is determined to discover who the culprit is behind the most recent highwayman ambush. And by catching the highwayman, she aims to persuade Sir John to bring his family, and his wealth, to her village. It may also make the handsome Moses notice her!

SARAH SWATRIDGE

TURPIN'S APPRENTICE

Complete and Unabridged

LINFORD
Leicester

First published in Great Britain in 2020

First Linford Edition
published 2021

A catalogue record for this book is available
from the British Library.

ISBN 978–1–4448–4731–4

Published by
Ulverscroft Limited
Anstey, Leicestershire

Printed and bound in Great Britain by
T J Books Ltd., Padstow, Cornwall

This book is printed on acid-free paper

Unwelcome News

Charity took another jug of ale to the table at the back of the inn. One man put out his arm to encircle her slim waist but she was too nimble for him and avoided his grasp.

The heavy oak door to the inn creaked open, letting in a blast of cold frosty air. Winter had started early and had been bitter.

'Over here,' her father called. He was holding yet another jug and nodded towards a group near the door. Business had never been so good and it was all thanks to Sir John and his family moving to the area and bringing the opportunity of lots of work with them.

Charity had never known the New Bell public house to be so busy. If business continued to grow like this she would have to ask Bessie to stay later, or even employ another kitchen maid. That would mean another mouth to feed and they already had Joe and Whistler, the stable boys.

There were several other inns and hostelries in the little village of Twyford because of where it was placed. Twyford was en route from London to Bath and many travellers stopped overnight, or to have a meal or collect fresh horses.

There was usually friendly banter between most of the publicans. The different establishments offered different things. For instance, the Bell on the corner was run by Widow Baldwin and she also had her own brewhouse. Her customers either liked or disliked her beer.

Strange as it seemed, Charity had never set foot in the Bell. Her father had banned all his daughters from doing so and he had changed the name of his inn to the New Bell just to annoy Widow Baldwin.

This had always puzzled Charity because her father was usually a kind and jovial chap, but the story went that she had been jealous of Charity's beautiful

mother who came from a genteel background. The women had never become
friends and this upset Charity's mother
which in turn upset Peter Bell.

Over the years Charity had heard other
versions of this story and she herself had
always greeted Widow Baldwin cheer-
fully and with respect whenever she saw
her in the market place.

The atmosphere at the New Bell was
full of laughter. All anyone could think of
was the good times ahead. Sir John had
already approved the plans to extend his
newly acquired manor. He was going to
use local bricks from nearby Reading
and bricklayers from the village. Later
he would need carpenters and the stone-
mason.

Once the manor was completely
restored they would need more domes-
tic staff to cater for his extended family
and once all that was done he could concentrate on the surrounding farmland
which meant work for the agricultural
workers.

Everyone would benefit, including

Peter Bell of the New Bell inn and his three daughters, Faith, Hope and Charity.

As much as Charity loved her two older sisters, at times like these when she was glad they were nowhere to be seen and she could shine in her father's eyes and become his favourite.

Hope, the middle sister, had managed to get herself an apprenticeship in the village with Mistress Brown, the milliner. Hope had made it perfectly clear she didn't want to spend her life serving in a public house.

Her plans were to learn the skills of a milliner so that one day she could set up her own hat shop in London and make posh designs for wealthy ladies.

The reality was that Hope was finding it much harder than she'd imagined. She was always complaining of sore fingers from all the sewing and already she'd found there was a great deal more to learn that she'd realised.

Hope was a dreamer who liked the idea of things rather than physically getting stuck in and working hard. Even her father admitted she was the laziest of the three of them.

However, she was always kind and gentle. Charity used a rag to wipe down a table and continued to think of her sisters. She'd not seen Faith since the previous evening when she'd overheard part of an argument between Faith and her father. He was generally an even-tempered man but something Faith had said, or done, had made him very cross.

'Get some bread and cheese for Master Brown.'

Charity smiled at her father, acknowledging his order, and refilled a jug of ale, setting it down beside him before slipping out the back to cut a few slices from a fresh loaf of bread.

'I'll have some if you've got any left,' Moses said with an easy smile.

'Out of my kitchen,' Charity told him, waving her arms about as though she were shooing out the geese. 'I've told you before, you're not allowed in here.'

'You never said that when I was a lad.' He laughed.

Charity tried not to smile at the memory of the scrawny boy who'd call in on his way home from Mr Polehampton's boys' school.

He and Charity had an unwritten rule back then. He would teach her what he'd learned that day in return for food. It meant that Charity was one of the few women in the village who could read, write and do her numbers.

Neither Faith nor Hope had the patience to try more than the basics but the more Charity learned, the more she wanted to know. The two of them had been inseparable since Moses had appeared in the village as a wee waif.

Now he'd removed his cap and stood with it awkwardly in his hands as he hovered by the back door, watching her every move.

'I have to speak with your father,' he said with some urgency. Suddenly his voice had become serious which made Charity look up.

She paused in her task and gazed at him hopefully. She often wondered if Moses had ever really noticed her, except perhaps as the sister he'd never had, and yet could he now be asking her father for her hand? Or was she being fanciful?

'He's busy in the bar serving drinks,' she told him. She hoped Moses would stay and chat with her. He did that sometimes and they always got on so well, she felt, although of late he'd kept his distance and she couldn't fathom why. 'He'll make time to listen to you, I'm sure.'

To her dismay, Moses disappeared back into the noisy public area of the bar, leaving Charity to guess what business he had with her father. She could feel her cheeks burning and was glad no-one was around to witness the redness that gave away her feelings for the handsome Moses Lamb.

Charity was just taking the loaf and cheese out to Master Brown when her sister Hope appeared at the door. No doubt she'd been out walking with one of the young men in the parish. Charity was not sure if she envied her.

Hope seemed to notice the lull in the hubbub from the bar at the same time as Charity became aware of it. She rolled up her sleeves ready to go and sort out yet another fight when Hope swept passed her, took the plate of food and slipped into the inn as though she'd been serving there all evening, leaving Charity to clear up in the kitchen.

'Food for the post boy,' her father called as he collected two more jugs from the wooden table in the corner. Hope passed the message on to her sister and then, like a ghost, she disappeared again. Charity had no idea where. It certainly wasn't back to the milliner's shop. More likely she had a hiding place with Faith and the two of them would be giggling together somewhere where they couldn't be seen.

Twyford and Ruscombe's population was about 600 at this time and Charity was convinced it was full of the most interesting characters. Being one of three girls she'd always been fascinated by three eccentric sisters who were now elders in the area.

Miss Rose was well known for growing roses in her home in Hurst, a neighbouring village. In summertime her gardens were full of colour and you could smell the perfume of the flowers lanes away … if the wind was in the right direction. Charity had always loved to visit Miss Rose and was often taken with her mother, who was also keen on roses.

Unfortunately Miss Rose had a sister living on the other side of Twyford. It was said they were inseparable as children but once Miss Rose had decided to grow roses they grew apart. Miss Violet, it seemed, disliked the flowers saying they made her sneeze.

For many years the sisters fell out over this and didn't speak, but when the third sister, Miss Marigold, married, the three of them came to an arrangement which was beneficial to the whole area.

The Flower Girls, as they were known, employed two young lads, Samuel and

Luke. All day, every day, these boys would travel back and forth between Miss Rose in Hurst, Miss Violet in Twyford and Miss Marigold, now Mrs Churchill, several miles away in Littlewick Green. The sisters would pass each other handwritten notes or verbal messages which the boys would deliver.

None of the Flower Girls had children of their own but they did realise that young boys needed to be fed and looked after if they were to perform their tasks properly, so Miss Rose, who knew Charity's mother, paid a regular monthly amount for the boys to be fed and occasionally housed at the New Bell.

The sisters realised that these two lads would occasionally be asked to deliver other messages for people and they allowed this, so long as their mail took priority.

The two young lads became regulars at the New Bell, calling in for refreshments and spreading the news and occasional gossip as they carried out their duties. No- one was interested in the petty messages that went between the three women but inevitably the boys heard what was going on elsewhere in the county. This happened about three times a day during the week but only once on Sunday.

The arrival of the 'post boys' meant regular income for the lively inn on the road out of town but perhaps more importantly than that, everyone knew they'd hear the latest news.

Charity and her father were well aware the arrival of these boys increased their trade. People were always keen to know what was going on in the surrounding villages and occasionally further afield.

'Highwaymen,' short Samuel said dramatically. He always liked to be the centre of attention but Charity knew to take his news with a pinch of salt. Samuel had been known to elaborate reports. In fact, he was so accomplished at embellishing a story, he could make even the most trivial of information sound like a Voltaire novella.

'Tell us more,' the landlord encouraged as he started a fresh barrel of beer, pouring one for the thirsty post boy. 'Was it on Hampstead Heath like before?'

'Sad to say it was closer to home,' Samuel continued. He took a long gulp of ale and let his words sink in before continuing with his information. He was the master of suspense. 'It was at the Thicket.'

Maidenhead Thicket was on the route to London and only a few miles from Littlewick Green and Miss Marigold's home.

'Not only that,' Samuel continued, relishing the attention from his audience, 'it was Sir John himself who was attacked.'

An eerie silence filled the inn. Everyone held their breath because the whole community needed Sir John to bring his family to the area and to settle. No-one could bear the thought that perhaps, just perhaps, something as awful as this could make him change his mind. No-one dared to think he might choose a different, safer village to make his home.

Charity looked over at Samuel. Reluctantly she admitted that on this occasion, she felt he was telling the truth, but perhaps it had been exaggerated. Maybe Sir John's coach was held up and threatened rather than him being robbed of his possessions. She could only hope.

'What was taken?' someone asked, while another person wanted to know if Sir John had been hurt and who else had been travelling with him at the time.

Charity breathed a sigh of relief as the inn became full of chatter and noise. Although, as she served refreshments, it seemed to her that all the conversation was speculation of some sort or another as to what had actually happened and how much of Samuel's story could be believed.

'Samuel,' she whispered as she cleared away his empty plate, 'you do realise the impact of your words? You must know how important it is for the village to have Sir John here?'

'What are you saying, lass?'

'How true is your story? Did you see it with your own eyes?'

'I don't just deliver mail here, you know. I stop at Littlewick Green and yesterday I took a message to a widow at Knowl Hill. They're all talking about it. Sir John's coach was stopped. He was held at gunpoint and he was robbed. Some say there was a struggle.

'I'll admit I don't think anyone was hurt more than a few bruises but they got away and no-one could really identify them. They wore masks, capes and a tri-cornered hat. The tall man who spoke, he wasn't local. It's thought he was a Londoner.'

Charity's heart sank. It seemed what Samuel was telling her was genuine. But by the time she reached the kitchen her optimistic nature had returned and she realised that this unfortunate event didn't necessarily mean Sir John would not relocate here. All was not lost and she would make sure she reminded everyone else of that. It was important to keep the customers happy. Without them, Peter Bell and his daughters could not survive.

Much later that evening, when it

was quiet and pitch black outside and only William Grant the night watchman walked the streets, Charity and her father swept up and cleared the inn.

Once again Hope was nowhere to be found when it came to tidying up. Faith was just the same. She'd not been seen all evening but there was nothing unusual in that these days. Charity's sisters both had high hopes of marrying well and leaving the inn, and possibly even the village, for good.

It was bitterly cold outside and there would surely be a frost come the morning. There was no sign of her sisters so Charity guessed they were curled up in the straw in the roof space above the horses in the stables. It was always warmer in there if you could put up with the constant noise from the horses and the smell.

'And what did Moses want to speak with you about?' Charity asked her father. 'It sounded as though it was something important.'

'Moses? I didn't see him at all tonight.

Are you sure he was in?'

'He was definitely here. He came to see me in the kitchen. Well, to be honest, he was looking for you. I sometimes wonder if he even knows I exist.'

'There's not a man in the whole of Twyford who doesn't know of you,' Peter Bell said proudly, giving his youngest daughter a rare hug. 'You're as beautiful as your mother and don't you forget it.'

Their mother, who had tragically died so young, had been the daughter of a local landowner. She had chosen not to marry for wealth as her parents wished her to do. Instead she married for love and it was Peter Bell the innkeeper who had stolen her heart.

As Charity fell into her own bed that night all she could think about was the warmth from her father's arms and the warm glow that perhaps Moses had noticed her after all.

Charity Makes a Deal

The following day they heard more about the highwaymen. This time it was from Luke, the other post boy. The two of them couldn't have been more different in looks nor in personality. Whereas Samuel was short and had a round belly, Luke was as tall as a lime tree. He was quiet and reserved. Charity suspected he was shy but he would happily chat to her if only the two of them were in the bar or if he'd brought his plate to the kitchen door.

It seemed Sir John, although greatly put out by the robbers, was made of stronger stuff and intended to pursue them in some way. However, his wife and daughters were considered delicate and for the time being it was decided they would stay where they were in London town, which came as a great blow to all the locals.

To add to Charity's woes, Moses

had come in early. He'd nodded in her direction, but hadn't smiled. He spoke earnestly with her father and then, his business done, he left without even a backward glance.

Charity now knew for sure he hadn't asked for her hand in marriage because she knew her father would have given his consent. He liked Moses, who was a quiet soul, and her father was well aware of her feelings for the young man.

'Out with it,' she demanded of her father. 'I saw Moses talking to you. You both looked quite solemn but I can't for the life of me think whose funeral you were arranging.'

'Brace yourself,' her father told her. 'You're not going to like it.'

Charity lifted her chin and put on a brave face, telling herself that nothing her father said would make her react.

'His folks have arranged for him to marry Molly Tanner. He came in to arrange for a couple of kegs of beer be put aside for their wedding.' Peter Bell reached out to hug his daughter but she bit her lip, shrugged and continued to stir a vegetable potage.

She turned her head away from her father so he couldn't tell how upset she was.

'There's someone out there for you, love, you mark my words. Perhaps you just haven't met him yet.'

'I don't want anyone else.' Charity sniffed.

'I thought you weren't interested in tying the knot. It's all your sisters ever talk about. I hoped you'd be the one to stay at home and look after me.'

'You don't need me to mollycoddle you,' Charity told him. 'But don't worry, I'll be here long after Faith and Hope have flown the nest.'

'Good - because we can take care of each other, can't we, love?'

'Of course we can,' she agreed as she fought back the tears that burned behind her eyes.

A cart trundled down the track beside the inn and her father went to investigate.

Charity stopped stirring the potage and took a few moments alone to feel sorry for herself. She allowed a trickle of hot tears to escape.

A few minutes later she splashed water on her face, gave it a good rub with her apron, stood tall with her shoulders back, ready once again to face their customers in the bar and to begin the sad state of putting Moses and her feelings for him safely away in her past.

She told herself she would never think of him again in a loving way, not now he was betrothed to Molly Tanner.

All the conversation that day had been about Sir John and the highwaymen. Some reports said it was just one man, while others talked of a whole gang who were armed and dangerous and, by some reports, were making their way slowly down the road toward the village in the direction of Bath.

'Here you are, Luke,' she said as she passed him a bowl of potage and a hunk of bread. She was glad the room was dimly lit and hoped no-one would notice her tear- stained face. 'Did you actually see anything yourself?'

'No, thankfully I was miles away.' 'So what do you think actually

happened?' she asked quietly as he blew on his hot food.

'I don't know that it was so bad,' Luke began. Charity could not believe what she was hearing.

'How can you possibly say that?' she gasped. 'It could have a devastating effect on the whole village.'

'I'm well aware,' Luke answered rather haughtily. 'But I rather think it has been blown up out of all proportion.'

'I can't believe I'm hearing this,' Charity told him.

'Let me finish, will you?' Luke snapped. 'Most reports, the reliable ones, anyway, talk only of one robber, masked and on horseback, with a pistol. All he took was Sir John's signet ring and some jewellery hc'd had made for his wife and daughters.'

'Are you sure?'

'I can't promise you it'll all blow over,

but some versions have practically an army of attackers taking all his possessions, and leaving Sir John and his men for dead at the side of the road. It's up to you what you believe.'

Charity poured some ale and looked thoughtfully at Luke who was now tucking into his meal.

'I suppose it isn't important what I think, or what anyone says. It's how Sir John feels and whether this incident will make him change his mind about coming to live here.'

★　★　★

That evening was noticeably quieter in the inn. Charity liked to be busy. Tonight it didn't matter at all that neither of her sisters were around. In fact, Charity thought, even her father could manage on his own.

The trouble was, if she had time on her hands she knew she'd end up day-dreaming about a rosy future, just her and Moses Lamb. But now that was never going to happen.

She decided she might as well catch up on some of the little jobs she rarely had time to do. She went to check the stock in the pantry, but even with a candle it was too dark to do a proper inventory. She'd have to do it first thing in the morning when the light was best.

She needed to know how much in the way of preserves they had left to last them until the end of winter. It was still only January, and because they'd had many months of cold weather already, their stocks were low, and she needed to know if she had to start rationing what was left.

As she was squinting at the produce and preserves Charity heard the unmistakeable sound of a carriage pulled by at least two horses. It was the sound of someone important. Few people had a carriage and it was the wrong time for the regular one that transported the rich from London to Bath and back. Charity's interest was piqued and she stepped out into the yard to get a better look.

The carriage stopped further down the road opposite the Dog. There were numerous inns in Twyford. Publicans all had other roles to play as well as running their drinking establishments. Her own father could turn his hand to many jobs. He could mend all manner of things which was usually what he did in the winter to supplement their income.

In the spring and summer he would become a farmhand and help with the harvest during the autumn.

The Dog, their nearest rival, had stabling for up to 40 horses and often housed the more well-to-do guests.

Charity nipped into the bar. Her father had everything under control and was chatting with Matt the baker, who had once saved Faith from being swept under a carriage when she'd been about three.

Charity slipped out and headed straight for The Dog.

'What you doing sniffing around here, missy?' one of the stable-hands asked her. Charity stood up tall and told herself that often, in her father's absence, she was landlady of the New Bell inn and therefore a woman of some standing and as such ought to be shown a little more respect.

She ignored his remark. 'Was that Sir John I saw arriving just now?' she asked.

'What if it was?' the stable-hand asked. It irked Charity that he could be so awkward when he had no notion of her business, and she was there to do her bit and save the village.

'Was it Sir John?' she asked again. 'He's in the bar,' a stranger answered.

The man looked her up and down. 'Who's asking?'

'Charity Bell, landlady of the New Bell inn over there. I'd like a minute of his time if I may?'

'Wait there,' the stranger replied. He re-entered the bar. Charity could hear men's voices but it was too dark to make out who was there. It didn't strike her as busy, and it heartened her that the Dog was equally quiet tonight. Then Charity heard a booming voice above the others.

'A wench wants to see me?' He laughed. 'Is she pretty?' There was a roar of laughter.

'Very,' the stranger replied and there was a round of applause, which made Charity blush and her heart beat more quickly.

'Then don't keep her waiting. Show her in.'

Charity took a deep breath as the man returned to fetch her. Her heart was pounding heavily beneath her bodice like it did when she had to stop a fight or throw out someone who couldn't take their drink.

Sir John, being a gentleman, stood and gave a little bow on her arrival. His companions looked surprised but they followed suit and showed respect.

'You wanted a minute of my time?' Sir John said pleasantly. He seemed in a jovial mood despite the recent attack. Charity didn't think he looked as though he'd been injured.

'Sir . . . ' she began. Her voice trembled at first but as she explained, openly and honestly, how important it was for him and his family to settle in Twyford, her voice became stronger the more passionate she became.

'You'll not find a place with so many hard workers ready to be loyal to their master, I promise you.'

'Quite a speech,' he said with a chuckle. 'And how many villages have you visited to know your men work harder and show more loyalty?'

Charity hesitated. She had never been in a position to travel. She had often been to Hurst with her mother to buy roses. Hurst was at least two miles away. It had seemed like an adventure.

For as long as she could recall she'd helped out in the inn, taking on more responsibility as she grew up.

'It's what I've learned from listening to the post boys,' she told him quietly but with confidence.

To her dismay Sir John laughed at her. 'You will have heard I was attacked on my journey here and goods were stolen. My wife is not strong and we have young daughters. I have no wish to put them in danger. You do understand that?'

'I do most certainly, sir. I have begun investigations to discover the culprits, and I intend to have them apprehended.'

'So you're not only the landlady of the New Bell but the local constable, too?' He laughed again.

'You'd be surprised what I hear when I'm serving ale,' she told him, determined to stand her ground.

'It's one thing to listen to gossip, but quite another to be able to prove any of it is true.'

'But I'm determined!'

Sir John gave her another hearty laugh. Charity sighed. The infuriating man just wasn't taking her seriously. She could see she was wasting her time, and his.

'Good day to you, sir,' she said and turned to go.

'All right, Charity Bell,' he called, 'I'll make a deal with you. You find and convict the highwaymen, making it safe for my family, and I'll promise you I'll proceed with my plans. These men will be my witness.'

Charity stopped in her tracks. She'd begun to fear he hadn't even listened to a word she'd said, but clearly he had.

She held out her hand as she'd seen many a man do, as they agreed on a deal. If Sir John was surprised, he didn't show it, but shook it. She could feel him watching as she left the dimly lit public house.

Standing Alone

Charity wasted no time in returning to the New Bell and engaging anyone and everyone in conversation about their knowledge of the local highwaymen.

'What makes you think he's local?' Luke asked her. 'Someone said his accent wasn't from round here. I heard he was a Londoner.'

That night as Charity fell on her bed of straw she lay awake despite being tired. Her mind was so busy going over everything she'd heard. The trouble was it was all conflicting.

She was almost convinced it was one man on his own until someone mentioned a gang all with masks and dark capes to hide their true identity.

She had no way of telling whether they knew the area well or if they had ridden all the way from Hampstead Heath to steal from the rich as they passed through the dense wooded area known as Maidenhead Thicket. Had it been a planned attack or were they just passing through and happened upon a wealthy-looking coach and horses?

Eventually she fell into a deep sleep. She dreamed of being on a carriage riding at the front with a gun of her own ready to protect Sir John's family all by herself.

Suddenly she felt the muzzle of a gun held to her head. She froze in panic.

It didn't go away, and eventually she became brave enough to open her eyes. The daylight was streaming through the crack in the wooden roof. She couldn't remember exactly what she'd been dreaming of until she felt something nudge the side of her head again and she feared, just for a second, that it was the muzzle of a musket or pistol.

In reality it was the damp nose of Moses's puppy.

'And what are you doing here?' she asked him. 'Am I going to have to take you back to your master again?'

Until now she had relished the thought

of an excuse to see Moses but now he was engaged to Molly Tanner she knew she needed to put a distance between them.

'Go away, shoo,' she told the dog.

He put his head to one side and looked at her as though he understood what she was saying, but not why she was behaving oddly. Usually she made a fuss of him and would feed him scraps before taking him back to Moses.

'Go,' Charity told him again as she rolled off the straw and ran her fingers through her hair.

The little dog continued to stay by her side as she fetched water and then firewood.

'For goodness' sake go home and leave me alone,' she told him.

'That's not like you,' a deep voice said, belonging to Moses himself. 'You usually greet me with a ready smile and treat Thistle as your own.'

'That's for Molly to do now,' Charity told him calmly before turning her back on her old friend and concentrating on gathering twigs to help start the fire. 'Please take your dog away and train him so he leaves me alone. I don't want him here any more. It isn't right.'

'And I thought you liked him as much as he obviously likes you.'

Charity bit her lip and wondered why Moses was making this more difficult for her. He seemed oblivious to the fact that she cared for him and to think she'd hoped he had feelings for her. How wrong had she been.

She could feel Moses watching her. She longed to engage him in conversation as she usually would, but as much as she cared for him, she vowed she would never take another woman's man.

Eventually she heard him call Thistle and together they disappeared off up the lane that ran alongside the inn.

Sad as she was, Charity gave a sigh of relief. It wasn't really in her nature to be aloof and unfriendly. She'd never be a good landlady if it was, but there were times when she had to discourage an unwanted suitor and now she had to discourage poor, gentle Moses, the man she'd loved for ever.

She set about her morning chores and then made her way into the village to find their local constable. Twyford was not a very large community and as far as Charity knew, the majority of its inhabitants were law-abiding citizens but for all that, the constable always seemed to be a very busy man.

She eventually found him on the green. He'd just released a man who'd had far too much to drink and had slept it off overnight in the lock-up. The man scurried off, holding his head until he reached the cattle trough where he splashed water on his face as if to sober himself up.

'And what can I do for you, Miss Bell?' the constable asked.

'It's what I can do for you,' she told him. 'I've made a promise to Sir John that I'll find the highwaymen who held up his coach and bring them to justice and once they're locked up he will move his family to the village. He promised and we shook on it. There were witnesses, too, if you don't believe me.'

'I see,' the constable told her, scratching his chin. 'And what has that got to do with me?'

'Well, you're the constable. What are you doing to find the villains and bring them to court?'

'That's not my patch,' he told her. 'I believe he was set upon at the Thicket. That's Maidenhead or Littlewick Green, depending where it happened. I can't cover everywhere. I don't even have a donkey!'

Charity could see she wasn't getting anywhere and she knew she needed the constable on her side rather than making him cross.

'That's where I come in,' she told him. 'I'd like to be your assistant. Imagine how pleased Sir John will be when we, or you as the local constable, apprehend the robbers and solve the crime so we can all sleep safely in our beds.'

'You only need to fear the highwaymen if you have a carriage and something worth stealing. Neither you nor I have either, so we can sleep easy.'

'But surely it's our duty to help others and you must know how important it is that Sir John and his family come here to live. Think of all the people he'll employ.'

'Miss Bell, your community spirit does you credit but it's all I can do to cover my small area. As much as I'd like to catch the criminals, there's nothing I can do unless they gallop through the village with the loot still in their possession.'

Charity looked at the constable who was now heading back to the main crossroads.

'I was thinking that perhaps we could set a trap to catch them.'

'I wouldn't advise that,' he told her. 'These men are dangerous. They carry guns and in some places they've killed people. Sir John was lucky no-one was hurt.'

'But even if we didn't set out to capture them straight away, perhaps we could watch them, and see what they were up to and either catch them red-handed or at least observe them so we can try and identify them. Maybe we could follow them and see where they live or where their base is?'

'Brave words, Miss Bell, and if I may say so, rather foolish coming from a young woman such as yourself.'

'But if you're not going to do anything about it, someone has to.'

'I can assure you that the constables and watchmen at the Thicket and in Littlewick Green will be doing everything to track these men down.'

'And what do you suggest I do in the meantime?' Charity asked him, standing with her hands on her hips, determined to get a satisfactory answer.

'I suggest, Miss Bell, that you return to your father and help him run his inn and leave me and the other constables to do our job. Now off you go before I put you in the stocks for loitering.'

Charity had no choice but to head for home, but she was determined not to give up. Constable Hargreaves had not heard the last from her.

★ ★ ★

On her way along the high street she noticed one of the men she'd seen with Sir John the previous evening. He was near the entrance to the Dog and seemed to be loading up a carriage.

'Excuse me, sir,' she said as sweetly as she could. 'Were you there with Sir John when he was attacked?'

'I certainly was,' the man told her.

'I dare say you heard me last night when I promised Sir John I'd find out who the man was and make sure he paid for his sins.'

'I did, miss, and it was a fine Christian thing for you to offer, but it's not a job for a lass.'

'Can you just tell me everything that happened that night? I've heard so many different stories and I really don't know which one is true but you were there so I'd believe your story.' Charity looked up into the man's face and gave him what she hoped was a winning smile.

'We were making good time, the horses were running well. It wasn't a full moon but there were a lot of stars, I remember, so we could see our way, otherwise we would have already stopped overnight.

'His lordship wanted to keep going although he had been advised to give the horses a rest.' He gave a sigh.

'All of a sudden we heard the sound of another horse and then someone shouted and told us to stop and for his lordship to get out of his carriage.'

'So was it just one person?' Charity asked.

'I only saw one man, but I think there were others taking cover in the trees. We did as he asked. Sir John, his servants and his men got out of the carriage and off their horses. The man with the gun remained on his horse but asked Sir John to remove his ring and to hand over a small box that he'd left in the carriage.'

'How did the robber know it was there? Or whether it was of any value?'

'I suppose he could see into the carriage from his horse as he was high up looking down. The man was watching everything that was going on. He took the box and the ring, fired one shot in the air which frightened all the horses except his own, and rode off into the darkness of the trees.'

Charity tried to picture the scene. She'd never been to the Thicket but knew of wooded areas and could imagine what he was describing.

'What colour was the horse?' 'Pardon?' the man asked, obviously surprised by her question.

'Would you recognise the horse? Did it have any patches or marks?'

'It was dark, probably black. I thought he was going to shoot us all. I wasn't looking at the horse. I wasn't feeling very brave, I admit. I was thinking of my mother and my sister and what they would do if I died.'

'And what did the man look like?' Charity continued. He shrugged.

'He had a dark tri-cornered hat, a dark

cape. I couldn't see a lot. A mask covered his face. It was a scarf or kerchief.'

'Was he fat or thin? Did you see the colour of his hair? Anything?'

'I think he was quite slight but he was clever and kept in the shadows. I wouldn't be able to identify him if I met him in the high street later this morning.'

'One last question,' Charity told him. 'What was his voice like? You said you heard him speak.'

'It wasn't very loud, not a booming voice, like Sir John's. I remember thinking at the time that he almost sounded like a gentleman because he spoke so softly.

'He addressed himself to Sir John, not to me. I really didn't hear much at all. I was standing well back. I didn't want to get involved. I've family to keep.'

'Thank you for your help,' she told him. 'If you do remember anything else, even the smallest detail, come and see me at the New Bell. I may even buy you some ale.'

At last, Charity thought as she returned

to the New Bell, now she was beginning to get a real picture of what happened that night, even though the details were a little on the vague side.

She busied herself in the kitchen, laying the fire and getting it to light. It was a job she did so often she no longer needed to think about it. Instead her mind was on other things.

More than ever she was determined to show Sir John, his men and the constable that she wasn't just Peter Bell's youngest daughter but someone as brave as Esther in the Bible. And just as Esther had saved the Jews, Charity would save Twyford.

In the winter evenings her mother would gather her three girls around her and tell them all the wonderful stories from the Bible. The story of Esther the orphan had always been her favourite and not only because of the fact that Moses was an orphan, too.

Charity rebuked herself for thinking, once again, about Moses Lamb. She would make him proud of her even if they could never share a life together, except perhaps as friends. She hoped this Molly Tanner knew how lucky she was to have captured Moses's heart.

'I'll show them,' she told Thistle the puppy who had wandered back into the kitchen looking for scraps. 'I'll solve the mystery of who these highwaymen are and I'll bring them all to justice, you see if I don't.'

'Too late, Charity Bell,' a voice said. It was Samuel the post boy. He'd just come from Miss Violet and was on his way to deliver a letter to Miss Rose. 'It's all been solved. The highwayman was none other than Dick Turpin and his band of robbers and thieves.'

Charity's Investigations

Charity shivered as she lay on her mattress of straw. It was already one of the coldest winters she could remember and tonight seemed to be the bitterest of nights.

If, Charity thought to herself, if the famous highwayman, Dick Turpin was the culprit in the recent attack, then I'll have to make sure there is evidence so that when he is brought to justice, he'll be given the appropriate sentence.

The trouble was, someone like Dick Turpin was so famous that people might even boast they'd been held up by him. So far, to her knowledge no-one had mentioned that Sir John had been accosted by anyone other than a common thief.

Despite Samuel being convinced of his guilt, Charity knew that Turpin would get away with it unless there was a reliable witness who could identify him and prove he was there.

She drifted in and out of sleep but awoke fully with a chorus of birds just as it was getting light. Inside her head she had more questions than answers. Despite her restless night she felt refreshed as she got up and went about her daily chores.

'They say Sir John was attacked by Dick Turpin,' she told her father as she served him porridge.

'Turpin?' Peter Bell said in surprise. 'Now that's a name I haven't heard in a while.

Your sisters loved to hear of his adventures.'

'He was a highwayman way back when I was a child, wasn't he?' Charity said aloud. 'But I don't really remember any facts about him. Does he live around here?'

Peter Bell stirred his porridge oats, the steam swirling up into the room at the back of the inn where he sat with Charity. In the background, Bessie swept out the ashes from the fire.

'Are you sure it was Turpin?' he asked.

'That's what Samuel said,' Charity told him. 'He gave me the impression he'd been

caught and was under lock and key.'

Her father took a mouthful of oats and looked up at Charity with a smile.

'You can't always believe Short Samuel, you know.'

'But others have agreed with him.'

'Turpin must be older than me!' Peter

Bell laughed. 'He was a legend when I was a lad, but don't believe what I say - go and speak to his aunt. She lives beside the church in Sonning.'

'Can you spare me for the rest of the day?' Charity asked, taking a mouthful of porridge even though she could see it was still too hot to eat. 'Bessie and the lads know what they need to do.'

'I'll manage, and I reckon it'll be quiet at the inn again tonight.'

'I'll be back by then, but I will go and see Turpin's aunt. She'll be bound to know if he's been caught and charged.'

Before long Charity donned her cape and headed for the Dog.

'You're going in the wrong direction,' her father called. 'Sonning's that way.'

'Trust me, I know what I'm doing,' Charity told him. 'I have a plan.'

As Charity left the warmth of the kitchen she looked around to check Bessie was doing as she'd been asked. She was a simple girl who worked hard but who needed to be guided.

The stable lads, Joe and Whistler, were busy in the stables grooming the horses.

A sudden movement caught Charity's eye. Faith's horse, Moonshine, was in the end stable and yet she didn't think Faith was at home.

It struck Charity as odd but she had no time to worry about that now. Instead she headed off up the road in the direction of the village. In fact, she thought, if Faith was around, she could muck in with the chores and that would ease the load.

There were a few stable-hands working with the horses at the Dog. Charity looked around for someone she knew but there were only the boys who mucked out the horses or groomed them and, despite their fanciful stories, she guessed they'd not travelled further than she had.

She had hoped to see Big Tom who ran the stables at the Dog. He'd been on many travels around the area and, if she was really lucky he might offer to take her over to Sonning on his horse but it didn't look as though it was going to be her lucky day after all.

At last she saw a familiar face, even if it was that of Moses Lamb. Charity took a deep sigh as she approached the man she was trying not to love.

'Good day to you,' he greeted her.

'I need to ask you a favour,' Charity told him, coming straight to the point. 'Can you tell me how to get to Sonning? I know the general direction but is there a river I need to cross?'

'I can do better than that.' Moses laughed. 'I have some deliveries to make in that direction. I'll walk most of the way with you, if you will have me as your escort?'

'I walk quickly,' Charity warned. 'I

hope you'll be able to keep up.'

'I'll do my best,' Moses said with a grin.

For a moment Charity could pretend it was just like the old days when they would go for long walks together and talk about a whole host of things.

'I've been hearing all sorts of things about you lately,' Moses told her. 'Someone even said you'd spoken with Sir John himself and promised to rid the town of its highwaymen.'

'That's true,' Charity told him. 'Sir John and I shook hands on the deal and I shall make sure Twyford is a safe place for us all, including, of course, Sir John's family.'

'So it's probably true what Constable Hargreaves said about you being his unpaid assistant?'

'I don't know what he's saying, but I did offer him my services if he would help me, although to be honest he wasn't at all keen.'

Moses paused and looked down at Charity. Even though they were the same age, Moses had always towered above her and vowed he would always protect her.

'And to think I used to fool myself that you needed looking after, when all along you're as strong as an ox, as cunning as a fox and as feisty as a ferret.'

'I can look after myself,' Charity agreed. 'But sometimes it would be nice to … ' Her voice trailed away as she remembered that Moses, her old school friend and confidant, was now betrothed to Molly Tanner and undoubtedly they would have to go their own ways.

They left Twyford behind them and headed down the lane and over the bridges toward the tollgate. A little way farther on they came to the water pump, only installed a few years ago but not needed to dampen down the road this winter as the road was either muddy or frozen.

'This is where I leave you,' Moses told her. 'Just follow this road until you come to the crossroads. The village of Sonning is to your left, this side of the river. The other side is Sonning Eye. You've gone too far if you end up there. Good luck with your enquiries.'

As Charity marched on, determined to reach the village of Sonning as soon as possible, she could feel Moses watching her. She turned and waved and sure enough he was still there standing by the water pump. He must be freezing, she thought. Charity wished he wasn't so handsome and now so unavailable.

Twice more she turned and waved, wishing he'd continue on his way. He'd told her he was calling in on Mr and Mrs Lamb, the kind people who'd taken him in when he was little more than a babe in arms.

The Lambs had been childless. The baby boy had been left in an Osier willow basket near the entrance to the chapel so they'd given him the name of Moses and cared for him ever since, although now of course, Moses was a grown man.

He continued to live with the Lambs at East Park Farm and often took their goods to market and at least once a week would call in with supplies for the New Bell.

As Charity continued on her journey she wondered what would happen once he was married. Would he stay on at East Park Farm or move to Wargrave where Molly Tanner came from?

Charity knew that if she wasn't concentrating on catching highwaymen, she'd be investigating the Tanner family of Wargrave, just to make sure they deserved someone as good and kind as Moses Lamb.

As Charity neared the little village of Sonning the road began to descend and suddenly the square tower of St Andrew's church stood only a little way off in front of her. She gave a huge sigh of relief and headed towards it but was distracted by voices and a hive of activity.

Charity had always been an inquisitive person. Neither of her sisters ever seemed to question anything but Charity was constantly asking why this, or why that? Sometimes her father despaired of her but she knew her mother was proud of her for 'having the inquiring mind of a boy'.

She took a left and wandered down a steep cobbled street to the Bull at the bottom of the hill, beside the church.

Charity smiled to herself for how better to find out exactly where Dick Turpin's aunt lived than to ask the publican?

'Go through the churchyard and take the path that leads up to the Bishop's Palace. Mrs Turpin lives in the cottage on your left.'

'Thank you,' Charity said. She shivered and pulled her cape around her shoulders. If she hurried she could speak with Mrs Turpin and then return in time for supper with her father. That was if Bessie had done as she'd been asked.

'Hello,' Charity called when she reached the cottage adjacent to the church path. 'Are you Mrs Turpin?'

'Who wants to know?' the old woman asked.

Charity explained her quest, being as sensitive as she could to the fact that the notorious Dick Turpin was this lady's kin. 'I don't know whether your nephew is innocent or guilty, but I just want to find the truth about who held up and robbed Sir John of his finery.'

'I can tell you it weren't our Richard and that's for sure,' Mrs Turpin told her. 'And don't think I'm just saying that because he's my brother's boy.'

Charity nodded but wasn't surprised the woman was protecting her family, she would have done the same.

'What makes you so sure he's innocent?' Charity asked quietly so as not to provoke the woman.

'Well, for a start, he's been dead and buried twenty years or so, God rest his soul.'

Charity gasped. She'd not been expecting this. Could the woman be lying or mistaken?

'He wasn't all bad, our Richard, he was always good to me, but he could be full of greed and that was his downfall.'

'And you're sure he's … no longer with us?'

'They passed the death sentence

on him in the spring of thirty-nine. A dreadful time for the family as you can imagine. We were all so ashamed of his wrong-doings, although I don't think he could have had the time to do all the things he's been accused of.

'I'm sorry to say my poor brother locked up his butcher's shop and travelled all the way to York, but he couldn't save him.'

Charity gently touched the woman's arm. 'I'm so sorry to have brought all this up

again. I didn't mean to upset you. At least I can say for sure it wasn't him who attacked Sir John recently.'

The old woman smiled.

'He was a good lad inside,' she said, 'and always had a good tale to tell when he'd call by. His lads are just the same, they can spin a yarn, believe me.'

'His lads?'

'Richard and Lizzie had three sons and a daughter. The eldest son became a butcher like his grandfather, but the other two are merchants, well pedlars really. They travel around buying and selling ribbons and the like.

'They always take good care of each other and if they are travelling nearby they call on their old great aunt.'

'I see,' Charity said, taking in the information.

'Now don't go accusing them of any wrong-doing. They are so ashamed of their father they won't even use his name.

They've taken their mother's name of Millington.'

'Christopher and Andrew Millington? I know them!' Charity said aloud. 'When they've been to market they always call in at the New Bell and try to sell their wares. I have bought a ribbon or two from them.

They look so alike — are they twins?'

'There's barely a year between them and even now I can't always tell them apart. 'Now don't go giving their game away and telling everyone they're related to a criminal who was hanged for his crimes. They're not angels themselves, but they'll not do anyone any harm, you can trust me on that.'

'Don't worry, their secret is safe with me,' Charity told her. She stayed a little longer helping Mrs Turpin with logs for her fire. It was going to be another cold night.

'I must be on my way,' Charity said at last. 'Thank you.'

As she was leaving, Mrs Turpin pushed a chunk of bread at her.

'I can hear your belly howling like a storm's brewing, so eat this and be on your way before the darkness sets in. I hate these short days.'

Charity thanked the old woman and as she made her way back to Twyford, she thought about all that Mrs Turpin had told her. In some ways she was no further forward. It meant that the highwaymen were still out there somewhere and could attack again. If they did, then that surely would be the end of Sir John's association with her home town.

Unexpected Guest

The candles had been lit and there was quite a bit of noise coming from the New Bell as Charity walked back up the hill to her home. She wondered what had happened to bring back their customers.

To her surprise not only was Hope serving drinks but her eldest sister Faith was stirring a cauldron of soup over the fire in the kitchen. So, it had been her horse, Moonshine, she'd seen out of the corner of her eye.

'Look what the cat's brought in,' Hope said as Charity arrived and headed straight for the warmth of the fire. It was beginning to snow.

'Faith!' Charity opened her arms to hug her sister. Faith spent most of her time these days away with a distant aunt who had offered to help refine the girls in order to improve their chances of making a good marriage.

Faith pulled back as soon as Charity

hugged her.

'You're freezing,' Faith said. 'Stand by the fire and warm up while I get you some food.'

Charity was so used to waiting on her sisters it was a pleasant surprise to have Faith wait on her.

Hope and Faith soon withdrew to the two wooden chairs by the fire and left Charity and her father to run the inn.

Each time Charity entered the kitchen and caught a bit of their conversation it was always about people she'd never heard of or the dresses they would be wearing to this event or that ball.

Charity considered herself fortunate. She owned two dresses, her work dress and her Sunday best — what more could a girl want? She had no time for silks or fine lace, as neither would be much use in the kitchen.

Once the last of the customers had gone, Peter Bell pulled the bolt on the door of his inn and went to join his three daughters in the kitchen.

'Well, it is a rare treat these days to

have you all here together and Faith, you're looking more like your mother every day. You're such a beauty.'

'Father,' Faith said seriously, 'I have some news.'

It appeared that despite Faith being an innkeeper's daughter, her aunt had managed, by some miracle to secure a good husband for her, if her father was in agreement. It was true, he wasn't perhaps a man Faith would have chosen, but he was comfortably off and Faith would not have to work as hard as Charity did each day.

'I'm sure we'll grow to love each other,' Faith said wistfully.

Charity tried to conceal a yawn. She'd been up early and, for the last half hour she'd been listening to her sisters discuss wedding dresses and spring flowers, even though no-one had actually been forward to ask their father for her hand.

'I'm going to bed,' Charity told them.

Just as Charity settled on her straw bedding, Hope and Faith came to join her. She sensed they would rather be sleeping in a four-poster bed with fine drapes and a servant to help them undress but here in the New Bell inn in Twyford a straw mattress was all they'd get but at least three bodies together would mean they'd be warmer tonight.

* ★ ★

Once again Charity woke early. The snow had fallen and the world outside was silent and white. For once Charity was warm in her bed and didn't want to leave it. Her sisters slept soundly, one either side of her.

She looked at Faith to see if she could see her mother's face, but Charity had only been eight years old when they lost her and the details of her mother had faded. All she could remember was her voice as she told them the stories from the Bible.

As she studied Faith's features, she recalled how Faith had always been somewhat of a tomboy. They'd all grown up in and around the local farms.

They had learned to ride, to round up pigs, to stack hay or chop wood. Charity wondered how Faith, or anyone, could settle for a life of sewing pointless tapestries or making idle gossip.

By lunchtime the following day the inn was quiet again. Not only had Faith returned to the genteel life with her aunt many miles away but she had taken Hope with her. Hope had been very keen to leave the milliner's and her departure would mean a chance for one of the village girls.

They had tried to persuade Charity to join them but she had no wish to marry anyone except for love and that didn't seem to be an option as far as her sisters were concerned.

'You could have gone.' Her father's voice broke in to her thoughts. 'I would have understood and your mother would have wanted you all to have been able to live a good life, one better than I can provide for you.'

'I'm happy here and I wouldn't think of leaving you,' Charity reassured her father. 'I'd look out of place in a silk gown when I'm stirring the soup!'

'So, if you're not going to live the grand life with your sisters and,' he paused, 'and Moses has other plans ... '

'I'll continue to solve crimes and I'll be the first ever lady constable!'

Just as Charity had spoken there had been a lull in the bar and some of the men had caught her last words. There were one or two sniggers and titters but no-one mentioned it to her as she collected plates and brought jugs of ale.

* * *

As Easter approached so, too, did Faith's wedding. Charity had hoped it would be at St Swithin's chapel in Twyford but it was to take place many miles away, amongst strangers.

'But I shan't know anyone,' she protested. 'I don't know how to behave in society and I've got nothing to wear.'

'They're sending a carriage to fetch us,' her father said. 'Faith said they would sort clothes for us and we would be told how to behave. It is only for a few nights and then we can have a carriage to bring us home again.'

Charity knew she had to do her duty and go to her sister's wedding. After all, she told herself, it would be an adventure, if nothing else.

Their adventure started as soon as they met the carriage in the courtyard at the Dog. Charity was glad to see she was treated with more respect on this occasion.

She recognised one of Sir John's men and was able to question him about the robbery.

'He sat proud and tall on that horse. It showed he had some breeding, he wasn't just a common thief,' the man told her. 'If your father doesn't object I could show you exactly where it took place, but have no fear, we travel in broad daylight and not even the most daring of criminals would risk robbing us today.'

Charity wanted to laugh because neither she nor her father had anything worth stealing and any highwayman would be disappointed.

Instead Charity pleaded with her father to let her sit up with the driver.

'How is it that one minute you want to be treated with respect and the next you wish to sit up-top beside the driver? It makes no sense to me,' he grumbled.

'At least let me sit with him until the Thicket and then I'll sit like a grand lady in the carriage with you for the rest of the journey.'

Her father considered the compromise and then nodded.

The spring had arrived at last but it was still cold. Charity wore her Sunday best and had a rug draped across her legs. She was still cold but was determined to sit it out and look for clues as they rode along the road to London.

'I want to know every single detail,' she told the driver excitedly. 'I'm trying to piece together the whole scene and solve the crime. I've promised Sir John and that's what I intend to do.'

'You're gutsy for a woman, I must say,'

the driver said.

They left Twyford and headed east towards Maidenhead. After a little while they joined a long dirt track. It went on further than Charity could see.

'This is the road,' the driver told her. 'Even the horses know which way to go now.'

Charity looked around her. She tried to think like a highwayman. She looked for possible places where he could hide so his attack would be a surprise.

'We're coming up to the Thicket now, miss.'

There were trees on both sides of the road. It wasn't a dense forest and in winter no leaves to hide behind. Nevertheless, if you had a dark-coloured horse and wore black clothes, it would be possible to hide behind the tree trunks in the shadows, especially at night.

From her lofty position Charity was able to form an idea of what it would be like for the highwayman to look down into a carriage. Would the coach driver have even known they were being watched?

The driver slowed the horses to a steady trot and then pulled them up.

'Are you riding in the carriage for the rest of the journey, miss?'

'Oh, yes.' Charity reluctantly had to agree but found her father sound asleep inside, although at least it was a good deal warmer than sitting up with the driver.

With no-one to talk to, Charity considered all the facts of the case. It had helped her immensely to see the very spot where the robbery had taken place.

Now she could picture it all in her mind but despite all this she was still no closer to finding out who might have been the culprit and the longer the time went on, the more unlikely it became that she would be able to catch the thief or thieves unless they committed a similar crime and still had Sir John's jewellery in their possession.

It was mid-afternoon by the time they arrived on the outskirts of London town, where Faith was to be married. Charity had not even met her future brother-in-law and above all she hoped he would be kind to Faith.

'He is somewhat older than Faith,' her father had said, 'but I found him to be a good man. I think he'll be the making of her, if he can tame her!' Peter Bell chuckled to himself but Charity wondered if there was a man alive who could 'tame' her sister.

Charity and her father were treated like royalty on their arrival, which certainly made Charity feel uncomfortable. She would rather have been made to feel like family.

Faith and Hope greeted them in the entrance hall which was larger than the New Bell inn and the Dog put together. 'You could stable twenty or more horses in here,' her father whispered as they stood in awe.

Charity hardly recognised her sisters. They wore elegant gowns and had refined manners. Both Faith and Hope wore little hats with net over their faces. Charity wondered if they were going out but it seemed they were not. Perhaps it was the fashion to wear headgear in the city, even indoors?

Charity thought Faith looked quite flushed, but her eyes sparkled with excitement and she was clearly glad to greet Charity and her father.

Charity felt she dare not even open her own mouth for fear of letting them down. Instead she just smiled and nodded and tried to copy her sisters.

'Let me introduce my fiancé, Mr James Hamilton-Smyth of London town,' Faith said, gesturing to a nondescript man standing beside her. 'And this is my youngest sister, Miss Charity Bell.'

Charity did a little curtsey which seemed to amuse James Hamilton-Smyth.

'I can see the family likeness,' he told her but then turned his attention to her father whom he'd met on one other occasion when he'd asked for Faith's hand in marriage.

As James and her father talked, Charity studied his face. It wasn't a handsome face but neither was it ugly. He was older than she had imagined and he looked troubled. Perhaps he felt out of place, too?

Her brother-in-law to be was fairly tall and looked well fed. He spoke with a quiet confidence. His voice was calm and pleasant and Charity wondered if she would grow to like this man if she were ever given a chance to get to know him.

They had just been seated in the drawing- room, awaiting tea, when they were distracted by a commotion in the entrance hall.

'What on earth is going on?' the master of the house, James's father, asked as he went to investigate. James followed in his father's wake, along with Charity and her father.

'It was an open road in broad daylight,' a large woman dressed completely in black was telling anyone who'd care to listen. She had a loud voice but for all her bustling and bravery she'd been scared by something.

'Whatever is the matter?'

'The Dowager and I were on our way here when we were attacked not a mile from your property. We were travelling with expensive gifts for the bride and groom, not to mention a wardrobe second to none.

They took everything.' 'On horseback?'

'There was one man, dressed from head to foot in black. I think there were others behind him because he kept looking over his shoulder, but only one man had the guts to come forward.

'He made us all get out of the carriage. We feared for our lives. Suddenly he shot his pistol into the air, the horses all reared up and raced off.'

Charity listened eagerly from the doorway to the drawing-room. The story was very similar to the many accounts she'd heard of the attack on Sir John. Perhaps the gang had not carried on to Bath after all but turned back towards London, if that was where they hailed from in the first place.

The guests were ushered back into the drawing-room and tea was served. Charity was just finishing her drink when the Dowager arrived, having freshened up. She demanded fresh tea and cake in her loud, booming voice. Charity assumed she was probably James's grandmother, or possibly an aunt.

She repeated her story. Charity listened attentively but learned nothing new.

'Would you be able to recognise the man on horseback?' Charity asked. Her father shot her a disapproving look but the Dowager was pleased to have such an interested party.

'I couldn't see much of him but I tell you when he leaned forward to speak to us, I reached out and scratched his face. He'll have a scratch, if not a scar, so he'll have to lie low for a while because that would help identify him.'

'Well done you for being so brave,' Charity told her, but was disappointed when Faith changed the subject.

Faith's Wedding

Later that evening, at dinner, a groom arrived with a message that was given to the man of the house, James's father. It wasn't until after the meal that Charity got to hear about its contents.

The carriage had been found only a mile away. It had been found ransacked. Not everything had been taken but again jewels were among the missing items. Fortunately, the wedding gifts and the Dowager's personal wardrobe of clothes were untouched.

There was nothing to say the highwayman had taken anything because once the carriage was abandoned, anyone could have dared to help themselves.

During the course of the evening Charity tried to learn more about the attack on the Dowager but each time she tried, someone stepped in and steered the conversation in a different direction.

Charity knew she should be making

polite conversation rather than speaking about the attack which was really all she wanted to know about. It was probably not considered polite to discuss such things over dinner.

It was a strange experience for Charity to sleep in such a grandiose room with a proper bed and a chamber pot. It was certainly warmer than the draughty loft space she usually slept in but that didn't ensure a good night's sleep. All she could think of was this latest attack.

The wedding took place the following day. Charity felt it was a very grand affair but Hope assured her it was a modest service and reception and when she married, which she hoped to soon, her wedding would be even more lavish.

Charity felt more than a little hurt not to be able to see Faith on the morning of her wedding. All she wanted to do was to give her sister a hug and comb her lovely long hair but she felt she was kept very much in the background.

The first time she set eyes on Faith, she was dressed totally in white. A veil covered her face and her dress sparkled with tiny beads as she walked down the aisle on her father's arm.

There was an elaborate meal afterwards. Charity spent the whole time trying to avoid talking to the many young men who kept attempting to engage her in conversation. She remained by her father's side and kept her mouth shut. She recalled the saying about the less you speak the more you hear.

In total contrast Hope danced with several young men and, Charity thought, looked comfortable and at ease talking to everyone she met.

'This is really not where I am meant to be,' Charity whispered to her father. 'I long to be back home in the kitchen at the New Bell. I never thought I'd say that but I'm even missing Short Samuel and his ridiculous stories!'

At the first opportunity Charity changed out of her borrowed gown. It was so heavy and awkward, it almost felt as though she had been set free once she'd discarded it. It was such a relief to shed the fancy clothes and to don her Sunday best which, she had to admit, was beginning to look a little on the shabby side but no-one in Twyford would have said a word.

A young maidservant had been assigned to Charity to help her dress and undress and to do her hair. Because Charity had slipped away at the first opportunity she found she was in her room alone. She'd never had anyone to assist her dressing and was therefore able to discard her robe on her own.

Having managed to slip away from the wedding party Charity watched as many people wandered around the beautiful grounds. She was happy to watch from the safety of her bedchamber window. Charity would have been happy to remain in her room but Hope sought her out.

'Come down and be sociable,' Hope invited her, 'but not in those old things. You'll need to wear the blue dress.'

'I'll just come down and wave Faith off and then I'll come back up here.'

'But you're too late,' Hope told her. 'She's gone already. There was a threat of bad weather so they slipped out as soon as the meal was over.

'But don't worry, she'll be back in a month or so after their honeymoon, and we'll come down to Twyford and visit. Well, we'll be staying in Sir John's house and you can visit us. I'll make sure to bring a gown for you to wear. You couldn't possibly be received in polite company in that.'

Charity stood up straight and proud in her Sunday best but Hope just looked down her nose at her.

'The sooner Father and I can leave, the better,' Charity told her.

'But I want you to meet Mr Mason. He seems to be very keen on me and he has a kind nature.'

'I hope you'll be very happy,' Charity told her sister and meant it, but nothing was going to keep her away from home longer than she had to be.

Hope swanned back out of the room and back to the wedding party. Charity could hear the music being played and would have liked to watch the events from the landing outside her bedroom but felt she might draw attention to herself.

She lit a candle sat and by the window to read but soon tired of her book. In an effort to pretend she was more ladylike than she really was, she had brought with her a sampler she had started many years ago and never finished. She sat with it now by the fireplace and tried to concentrate on doing a few cross stitches.

When she looked up she noticed a door beside the fireplace that must surely lead into her sister's bedroom. The three girls had all been allocated rooms along the same corridor. Of course tonight, Faith would be elsewhere on the estate or wherever her new husband had taken her for their honeymoon. Charity prayed he would be kind to her and treat her well. She was disappointed not to have been able to wave her goodbye.

She stood and stretched before going to investigate the handle of the door. It was locked but then she found a key on the mantelpiece and tried it. The door swung open and she found herself gazing into Faith's bedchamber.

Charity turned to fetch her candle.

Carefully she carried it into Faith's room. No fire had been lit because no-one was expected to use the room that evening.

However, there was a bright moon outside and the drapes had not been drawn so the moonlight lit up the room and cast eerie shadows all around.

Charity stroked the covers on the bed but they did not remind her of her sister. She tried the chest but it was full of beautiful gowns which she had never seen before, although she guessed they now belonged to Faith or would be passed on to Hope.

As a last resort Charity walked over to a small table with a mirror. This is where a maid would comb Faith's hair, she thought. There were two drawers either side of the table. Charity gently pulled at one of the drawers. It was empty except for a pale yellow ribbon.

It made her think of Andrew and Christopher Millington and the ribbons the pedlars sold as they went on their travels keeping the secret of their true identity with them.

The other drawer, however, was locked, or stuck. Charity knew she ought to return to her own room and prepare for bed.

She rattled the drawer but couldn't open it. She searched in the open drawer with the ribbon and pulled it out to tie it in her hair. To her delight on the end of the ribbon dangled a small key.

It opened the locked drawer and inside was a little pouch that she knew belonged to Faith. Their mother no longer had any fine jewels to leave her daughters but she had been given some lacy handkerchiefs which she had made into three little bags or 'pockets', one for each of her daughters.

Charity was surprised Faith had left it behind but then no doubt she would return to this house, if not this room, at some point in the future and retrieve her belongings. Charity guessed she'd probably get a maid to clear the room on her behalf.

Inside the muslin bag was a ring. It was large and gold and unfamiliar. Charity tried it on but it was far too big for her dainty fingers. It looked more suitable for a man.

Charity heard footsteps coming along the corridor. Quickly she replaced the bag with the ring, locked the drawer and left the ribbon with the key in the opposite drawer and vacated the room.

The footsteps continued down the corridor. Charity gazed out of her window at the moon for some time. It gave her comfort that she could stare at the moon and somewhere, miles away, perhaps Moses was looking up at the same moon and would think of her.

But then she recalled that if he thought of anyone, then he would think of Molly Tanner rather than his old school friend and confidante. She chided herself for allowing such thoughts of her old love

Moses, but would it ever get any easier for her?

A short while later Charity heard two sets of footsteps again. This time she went to the door wondering if it were her father and Hope coming to wish her a good night's sleep. Looking through the keyhole she spied two maids.

She envied them because they were standing on the hallway that looked down on the dancing below. It was like a balcony that went round the whole of the second floor. Charity would love to go and join them and watch the dazzling guests but knew she would not be accepted by the maids.

Just as she was about to move away from the door she caught a snippet of their conversation. They were laughing at the odd behaviour of her sisters.

That's a strange one if ever there was.'
'Part witch if you ask me.'

'She wanted me to find her the biggest cobweb I could!'

'She asked me for butter and then rubbed it on her face!' the other maid said and they both giggled.

Charity decided she had heard enough. She stood up and purposefully dropped her book on the floor. Almost immediately she heard two sets of footsteps pitter-pattering down the corridor and back to the servants' quarters.

She knew her sister to be no witch. Neither Faith nor Hope was practical or sensible, but there was not an ounce of evil in either of them.

Nonetheless, it did trouble Charity. She tried to convince herself that this peculiar behaviour was Faith's attempt to make her skin look firm and beautiful for her wedding day, and what girl wouldn't try anything, however absurd, to look her best for her intended?

Saddened by these thoughts, she prepared herself for bed and was surprised to find she fell asleep almost instantly.

As it happened, because of the attack on the Dowager in broad daylight, it was decided Charity and her father would outwit the highwaymen and leave immediately after breakfast the following day.

Neither of them had a great deal of luggage so there was only a minimal amount to pack up.

Once again, Peter Bell nodded off to sleep almost as soon as the carriage journey began. Charity amused herself by watching the world go by from the safety of her warm carriage seat but the countryside was very similar and soon she found herself trying to solve a mystery.

Charity gave a little shiver. Something just did not feel right but she was not sure what it was. She thought again about the wedding. Faith had seemed very happy. She certainly looked beautiful. Hope had come to wave them off but Charity noticed how tired she looked and how she had not eaten any breakfast. Perhaps she had gone to bed too late the previous night.

As they reached the Thicket, the road and surrounding area began to look more familiar, Charity felt a little lighter. She had never realised how important her home and the neighbours around her were to her. The women would all want to hear every detail about Faith's wedding and about Hope's prospects for a new husband.

Unrest

Charity had never felt so pleased to be in her own kitchen. It felt right - she had not been able to be herself during the whole time she was away. Sadly she admitted both her sisters had changed into smart young women who looked the part of real ladies, but it broke her heart that they no longer seemed like her sisters who would have laughed when they ran in the field or made daisy-chains or picked the wild flowers. Were those happy, carefree days gone for ever?

The inn was busy. There was a lot of unrest. The men were angry and tempers were rising, and Charity knew she had to be on her guard. She had learned from experience that the best way to deal with men who fought was to nip it in the bud almost before the fight began.

Her light-hearted humour was often enough to defuse a quarrel, and tonight she would need to keep her wits about her.

The anger was not aimed at her or her father. People were unhappy about the Turnpike. They paid their toll and all the men, rich and poor alike, had to do their four days a year of road maintenance. Of course, those who were rich enough, paid other men to take their turn. However, it seemed the roads were not being kept in a good enough condition.

Only last week one man had lost his load of goods because there was a hole in the street which damaged his wheel. The wheel came off his cart and the goods he was carrying fell to the ground. Many things were spoiled because of the mud on the road and the dust.

'Fire!'

Charity looked up.

'Fire!' the man's voice shouted again. 'Keeper's Cottage is alight!'

There was a mass exodus from the inn. People crowded further on down the road nearer to the tollgate and the Keeper's Cottage. Charity could smell the smoke in the air.

The closer she got, the more the smoke began to irritate her eyes. She could see the flames now and hear the crackle of the wood burning.

The tollgate keeper lived in the cottage with his wife and their five small children. She said a prayer for them, hoping they were all away from home.

A team of men were working together to make a chain, passing a barrel of water from one to another in order to douse the fire. Charity stood and watched in horror for a short while and then something stirred inside her. It was no use her watching, she needed to help.

She ran back to the inn, fetched a wooden bucket and hurried back to the scene of the fire where she started up a second chain dunking the bucket in the Old River to try and extinguish the blaze.

It took another hour before it was under control and several more hours before the flames were all out. The cottage was just a burnt-out shell but at least, miraculously, none of the family had been hurt.

A few of the men had been affected by the smoke they'd inhaled but the only person to have been burned was Moses. He'd been on his way into Twyford from East Park Farm where he lived.

He'd noticed the flames and had entered the house in order to alert the family. He'd helped rescue all the children but in doing so had hurt his arm - the skin was red and raw.

'Let me help you,' Charity said as she led him slowly back to the inn. Her mother had taught her which herbs to use to ease a host of ailments.

As they neared the inn Charity caught sight of Bessie.

'Make up a bed for Moses, he's been hurt and we need to treat his injuries.' Immediately Bessie scurried off to do as she'd been bid.

'Kneel here,' Charity told Moses. They crouched together near the stream that ran down to the river near the mill. Charity scooped up handful after handful of the cold water to dampen down the heat from the burn. 'Sorry if it hurts but it will help it heal.'

'I trust you,' Moses told her.

After some time Charity held her hand just above his arm. She could no longer feel the heat so intensely.

'I think we may have got the worst of it,' she told him. 'Now come with me and I'll make you a poultice.'

Charity used oatmeal and cold water to make a poultice and then told Moses to rest. She suspected he was suffering from the shock of it all. He was used to being on the go all the time but he made no objection and did as she asked.

'Sleep well and I shall bring you food in the morning,' she told him.

Just as she was leaving, their eyes met. They didn't say anything, there were no words that needed to be said. Charity sensed there was a love between them but one that could only ever be the love of a brother and sister. She lowered her eyes.

'Goodnight. God bless and keep you safe.'

Charity was up bright and early the following morning. The sun was shining and she felt the warm rays on her face as she went about her chores. Summer was definitely on its way and despite the previous day's events she felt a certain cheerfulness.

It was then that her eyes spied a little clump of viola, or heart's ease. The pretty purple and yellow flowers were lovely but today it made her wonder if there was ever a cure for a broken heart.

In the background she heard Bessie clattering about in the yard. It brought her back to her senses. She had things to do and she went out in the little garden in order to dig up a new potato. She needed one for Moses's minor burns.

'Good morning,' Constable Hargreaves said, making her jump. 'Just the person I was hoping to find.'

'Really? What is it I can do for you, sir?' 'I'm investigating the business of the fire at the tollgate yesterday. Do you know who started it?'

Charity knew that if she'd been in the inn more the previous evening she might have heard what was being said but she'd spent more time looking after Moses and their paying guests.

'I haven't heard any names mentioned,' she told him, 'but I will listen out and let you know what I hear.'

Constable Hargreaves looked at her long and hard as though he were trying to work out whether she was hiding any information from him or not. He seemed to be happy with what he saw in her innocent face, nodded and moved on.

Good day to you, Miss Bell.'

Charity dished out bowls of porridge oats. While they were cooling down she went to check on Moses.

'Good morning,' she called from outside his door.

'It's all right, you can open it. I'm up and dressed.'

'Well, that's good news,' Charity told him as she went to inspect this wound.

'The water and the poultice have taken the heat out of it, but you need to make sure you keep it clean.'

'Not easy when you work outside most of the time.'

'True, but you would find it even more difficult if you lost your arm due to infection. So look after it and if you're not going to, at least let me check on your arm from time to time to make sure it continues to heal well.'

'Yes, Dr Addington.' They both laughed at the in-joke. Dr Addington had been a local doctor who was now reportedly looking after very distinguished gentry, some even said King George himself.

'You have some minor burns as well. When you've eaten your porridge, I'll rub a potato on them and that will help.'

'What would I do without you?' Moses said lightly but looked up at her with tenderness in his face.

For a moment Charity wondered if he was going to take her into his arms and kiss her. Fortunately her father called from the yard and she hurried down to see what he needed.

Once Charity had seen to her father and collected the eggs she returned to the kitchen for her breakfast. As she did so she caught the tail end of a conversation between Moses and her father.

'He wasn't a man I instantly took to,' her father was saying. 'He was nearer my age than hers, but so long as he is a good husband to Faith, I'll have no reason to fault him.'

'But sir, would you consider any man good enough for one of your girls?' Moses said it lightly and the two men chuckled.

Moses left soon afterwards. Charity knew he had no choice. He had work to do. She and Bessie had the daily chores to complete, too.

That evening, the inn was quiet and her father had just finished his meal.

'Do you know of Moses's plans?' she asked. 'I mean, does he intend to move to Wargrave?'

'You need to ask him, not me,' Peter

told her. 'But I can't see him leaving the Lambs. They rely on his help. I think it's more likely the lass will move in with him at East Park Farm.'

'But I heard she had no brothers to work the family farm.'

'That may be the case but Moses is a loyal lad and Mr and Mrs Lamb have been good to him. One day the farm will be his, no doubt. He'll want to make sure it's all in good order.'

The inn started to fill up and Charity was kept busy. She made sure she listened carefully to what was being said. Constable Hargreaves wanted to know any snippets of useful information about the fire and she still had at least one highwayman to catch.

A New Role

Luke the post boy stood almost as tall as the doorway. His frame blocked out the light and made Charity look up.

'There's a letter for you. Well, it's addressed to your father, but ... '

'Give it here,' Charity said. They both knew her father couldn't read.

Charity took one look at the handwriting on the envelope and knew it was from her sister Hope. She had never been eager to learn her letters. It had always surprised Charity that out of the three of them, Hope could sew the neatest stitches and yet her handwriting was large and ungainly.

She tucked the letter in her apron pocket and made sure Luke had bread and ale.

Several of the tables needed clearing in the bar so she set about tidying the place up.

There was a small group of men in

one corner, deep in conversation but as Charity came within earshot they went quiet.

At first she wondered if it were just coincidence and so she moved right away and they began to talk again. She left the inn and went round the side of the building to a window near where the men were sitting.

The window wasn't open but it had never fitted properly and let in a draught of cold air. It also meant she could quite clearly hear what was being said.

'It's simple, really,' a man with a deep voice was saying.

'Simple if you've got a horse and a carriage and something worth stealing.'

Unfortunately Joe chose that moment to lead a couple of horses out to the road. The noise their shoes made on the cobbled stones and the neighing sound as they waited impatiently meant she could no longer hear what was being said.

It was some time later when Charity got to sit down and read Hope's letter. Her handwriting was appalling, but the gist of it was that she was hoping to marry Rev Mason and would like her father to come up to town.

Charity sighed. Hope sometimes thought the whole world worked around her and she would expect her father just to leave the inn, which was his livelihood, in order that he could make an expensive and dangerous journey just on the off chance that he might meet this Rev Mason and that, if this man was actually interested in her, he might ask for her hand.

Charity re-read the letter. She tried to consider whether a man of the cloth was the right choice for Hope who could be a free spirit.

Hope's postscript troubled her even more. It suggested that Rev Mason had a suitable cousin who had shown more than an interest in Charity whom he'd seen at a distance at Faith's wedding.

That evening the inn was busy. They had people staying which made more work for Joe and Whistler in the stables and for Bessie.

Charity kept her wits about her as she served drinks and food. From what she gathered there was still a lot of bad feeling surrounding the tollgate because people were using the road further down and then bypassing the tollgate to avoid having to pay.

The people of Twyford blamed the villagers from Sonning and no doubt the Sonning residents blamed those from Twyford.

'It's just not fair. We pay the toll and we have to mend the road. They use it just as much as we do.'

'Has the tollgate closed down now after the fire?' Charity asked.

'No, he's still there with his family, they just haven't got a roof. I heard he caught trespassers building a bridge across the stream so they could avoid the toll. It turned nasty and later that evening they must have returned and set fire to his place.'

'At least no-one was killed,' Charity reminded them. 'Do you know who it was?'

'The toll-keeper isn't saying a word. I suppose he's worried what would happen next.'

Charity took the empty jug from their table and moved on. Later Constable Hargreaves called by. He said it was to check the ale to make sure they weren't diluting it with too much water.

'Can I have a quiet word?' Charity asked him as she poured him a jug of ale. She relayed the story of the toll-keeper's plight. 'Have you spoken to him?'

'Of course, he was the first person I interviewed.'

'He's scared they'll come back and hurt his family. Can you offer him any protection?'

The constable thought for a little while as he sampled the beer.

'Perhaps if I caught them red-handed crossing the stream or even building another bridge, I could at least have them for trespass and if the toll-keeper would then come forward then maybe we could bring them to justice.'

'It won't give him a new roof, though.'

It wasn't until much later that Charity had a chance to speak to her father about Hope's letter. She failed to mention Mr Mason's cousin.

'I do have some business I could do in London,' her father said to her surprise. 'You'd be able to manage here, wouldn't you?'

'Not if it's as busy as it was tonight,' Charity told him. 'And we had Constable Hargreaves in checking the quality of our ale.'

'I'll go after May Day,' he announced. 'Will you write to Hope and let her know?'

Charity sighed but knew she had no say in the matter, although she would make sure Hope was aware that she had no wish to marry anyone.

* * *

The following morning, Joe and Whistler were loading up a cart with several barrels of beer to be delivered around the area. It was the end of April and villagers were preparing for the forthcoming May Day celebrations. There would be dancing, drinking and merriment.

Charity noticed Constable Hargreaves heading off down the road toward the toll gate. He was accompanied by the surveyor who made sure that each and every man took his turn in repairing the roads and maintaining the ditches.

The surveyor was not a popular man. He kept thorough records of which men had done their stint and for how long. He wasn't open to bribes although the wealthier residents did pay their workers to stand in for them.

It was a busy time in the kitchen as Charity and Bessie had lots of extra food to prepare for the May Day trade.

Constable Hargreaves dropped in again some time later with a big smile on his face. Charity was pleased for the excuse to leave the kitchen and to speak to him.

'You did well to tip me off the other evening,' he told her. 'You got me thinking and we set a trap. We caught the blighters red-handed and the toll-keeper is going to testify against them.'

'That's excellent news,' Charity told him. 'It was your idea to set a trap.'

'It was, but you played your part and,' Hargreaves paused a moment, 'you'll be pleased to know the surveyor is ensuring the men who repair the roads also repair the cottage. The squire has offered to pay for building materials in lieu of doing the manual work.'

It was Charity's turn to smile.

'Thank you for letting me know that. I was worried about the family and how they would survive if we had another wet spell. And the April winds can be really bitter.'

'They'll be fine and they were grateful for the food you sent down with Bessie.'

'It was the least I could do.'

'And so this is for you.' Constable Hargreaves opened his hand and held out a penny. 'I can't officially call you my assistant on account of you being a lass, but you and I can have an agreement and it could work to our advantage if you are working undercover, as it were.'

Charity took the penny and popped it in her apron pocket quickly before anyone could see. No-one argued with Constable Hargreaves, so she didn't try but she would continue to help him keep law and order in Twyford.

As soon as she could, Charity darted up to her room. Hidden in the darkest corner she had a wooden box in which she kept her most prized possessions. She had a lock of her mother's hair, and the muslin bag made from her mother's lacy handkerchief, a button from Moses's coat and her Bible.

Now she added the penny.

She returned to the inn feeling pleased with herself even though it had to be a secret between her and Constable Hargreaves but she could live with that, at least for the time being.

Seeing the button in her special box brought Moses back into her mind. She'd not seen him for a couple of days and wondered how his burn was doing. She was surprised to see Mr Lamb ordering a jug of ale. She was about to ask him how Moses was when her father reached out and stopped her.

'The wedding's tomorrow,' he said quietly in her ear. 'Best keep your thoughts to yourself.'

* * *

May was Charity's favourite time of the year. She loved nothing better than walking through a wood of bluebells. She loved to see the cherry trees with their bright pink blossom and hear the birdsong as they made their nests and fed their young.

However, her mood was dampened by the thought of Moses marrying Molly Tanner today of all days . . . May Day.

It helped that the inn was full, the weather was good and the majority of people were in a festive mood. The takings would be good today and would see them through the leaner times.

'Aren't you going to watch the maypole dancing?' her father asked when there was a lull after the midday rush.

'I've sent Bessie and the boys to go and watch. I'll clear up here.'

Once she had tidied up she sat and wrote a quick note to Hope explaining that her father would come and visit her but she need not trouble herself trying to find a husband for Charity as none was required.

Charity sealed the note and put it on the dresser until either Luke or Samuel arrived. Hopefully one of them would be able to hitch a lift on a carriage and deliver it.

Charity sat in the sunshine and closed her eyes, enjoying the warmth of the sun on her face. When she opened her eyes a little while later she thought she caught a glimpse of what looked like Mr and Mrs Lamb heading down the road out of town back towards their farm.

She couldn't dwell on it because she heard Bessie's footsteps on the cobbles and her loud voice calling.

'Charity! Charity!' The only person with a voice as loud as Bessie's was her sister Faith who could sing at the top of her voice if she thought no-one was listening.

'You'll never believe it,' Bessie told her. 'She didn't come.'

'You're not making sense,' Charity told her. 'Who didn't come? The May Queen?'

'No, the girl Moses was to marry. She's disappeared and run off with someone else. Everyone was furious and Moses has gone into hiding.'

'So it was the Lambs I saw walking home,' Charity told her. 'I thought it was odd to see them so early in the day. I thought they would still be dancing and drinking ale.'

'Her parents were so embarrassed by her behaviour they told all the guests to eat the food and drink the wine but the musicians were sent away and there was no dancing.' Charity thought back to Joe and Whistler loading up the barrels the previous day. She hadn't realised some of that beer had been

destined for Moses's wedding party.

And what a perfect day to be married, but it was not to be. Not for Molly and Moses and not for her.

'I wonder how he's feeling?' she said aloud, not expecting Bessie to be listening. 'He'll be glum for a day or two and then he'll pull himself up, dust himself off and get on with life. Moses does that.'

For Bessie this was a long speech. Charity looked up at her. Bessie was a simple girl. She was often teased because she claimed to speak to the dead, whereas all she was doing was giving a comforting word to a widow or grieving mother.

'The wedding was never meant to be,' Bessie told her but didn't go on and offer her any other words of hope or comfort.

They were joined by Joe and Whistler who'd clearly had more ale than usual. 'You should have come,' they told Charity.

'Bessie's already told me about Molly Tanner running off with someone else.'

The boys looked at each other as though this was news to them but they weren't really very interested.

'There's been another robbery,' Joe said. 'A highwayman held up and robbed some gent. It was near the Bowl and Pin.'

'Really?' Charity asked, looking up at the two stable-hands. 'Are you sure? In broad daylight and on May Day when there's so many people around?'

'No, it was last night. The gent was coming down the road from Ruscombe and was stopped. He had to hand over a gold watch and chain which had been given to him by his father.'

'Who was the gent?' Charity asked.

The boys shrugged and went to sleep off their afternoon activities.

The inn was quiet. Most people were still congregating down by the village green.

Charity let herself be persuaded by her father to at least take a walk into the village to see for herself.

Charity had no interest in watching the maypole dancing on this occasion. She headed straight for the fork in the road and the Bowl and Pin.

'He might have been rich but he was a

fool,' the landlord told her. 'Last week he was in here and he was showing off this gold watch. We all knew it was in his possession. No wonder someone thought to take it from him. It was his own fault.'

'And who was he?'

'I don't think he gave his name,' the landlord continued, 'but he was dressed in all the fine clothes. There was something strange about him though.'

'Strange?'

'I can't tell you what, but I never trusted him. Something wasn't right about him, that's all I can say.'

Charity strolled back toward the green heading for home when she came across Constable Hargreaves.

'It isn't a crime,' he told her before she'd even had a chance to open her mouth.

'He was attacked by robbers and had his gold watch stolen!'

'Oh, I thought you meant Miss Tanner jilting Moses at the altar.'

'Have you seen Moses?' Charity asked quietly. 'I heard he'd gone into hiding.'

'If I know him he'll be back at the farm working quietly away building a new chicken house or chopping wood. Give him some time and he'll find you, no worries on that score.'

Charity blushed as the realisation that it seemed everyone in the whole of Twyford appeared to know of her feelings for Moses except the man himself who had always treated her as a sister.

'Now, tell me more about this gold watch,' he asked. 'Did you say it had been stolen?'

Charity told him all she knew and was amazed he knew nothing of the case.

However, he was aware of a gold pocket watch on a chain having been stolen some weeks ago from a man in Hurst.

'I smell a rat,' Constable Hargreaves told her, 'and I intend to catch the rat. No doubt you'll be able to help me again. Keep your eyes and ears open and I'll come for a pint at your inn when I've heard a bit more.'

Constable Hargreaves tapped the side

of his head and went in the direction of the Bowl and Pin. Perhaps he was going to check whether they ever watered down their beer or whether they were aware of any suspicious behaviour?

Left in Charge

'I'm leaving you in charge,' Peter Bell told Charity. 'You know who you can call on if you need any help. I'll be back by the end of the week. I'll give your love to Hope and to Faith if I see her.'

'Yes, give my love to Hope but on no account are you to bring me back a husband!' Charity laughed and kissed her father before he left to pick up the carriage that would take him all the way to London.

That evening there was a steady stream of customers but Charity felt she had everything under control. Bessie was glad to earn a bit extra helping out in the kitchen and Joe, being the bigger of the two boys, was on hand to help with the barrels or if there were any signs of trouble. Meanwhile Whistler saw to the horses in the stables.

Charity had her eye on the man in the corner of the room. He wasn't a local and he'd ordered ale an hour ago and was making it last. He sat alone but was obviously listening to all that was going on around him.

She'd heard from Constable Hargreaves that highwaymen often hung around the pubs and inns listening out for someone who was travelling with a precious load. This man had made her suspicious. Perhaps he was the very man who had robbed Sir John and maybe even the Dowager on the day before Faith's wedding?

'Anything else I can get you, sir?' she asked but he just shook his head. He didn't even look up at her but Charity made sure she got a good look at him.

Not only that but she'd pointed him out to Joe who also made a note of what he looked like. They were fairly confident they would know him if ever he were to return.

'Joe,' Charity said, 'I've seen you sketching. Go and fetch your charcoal and make me a sketch of this man. I need a true likeness so that if we had to show it to Constable Hargreaves he would then be able to recognise him. Do you understand me?'

'Yes, Miss Charity.'

Joe discreetly sat behind the bar and sketched the stranger sitting at the table.

'That's very good,' Charity told him as she slipped him a coin. 'I don't want to lose you, but you're wasted here as a stable- hand. Don't you ever wish for something more?'

'I'm happy here, miss. I have a bed to sleep on, food in my stomach and Whistler's like a brother. We look out for each other. I can't imagine any other life.'

The following night the inn was deserted. 'Where has everyone gone?' she asked and tried not to think that the men of the village had chosen to drink elsewhere because she was running the place instead of her father.

'Don't fret yourself, miss,' Joe told her. 'I hear they're racing ferrets and there's lots of money changing hands.'

'Constable Hargreaves won't like the idea of gambling on his patch.'

'I dare say he won't ever get to know about it,' Joe told her. 'The least you know the better.'

He winked and Charity decided that perhaps she had better not question him too much more or she could alienate her customers for good and then she and her father would have no livelihood left.

The evening began to drag. Charity realised she liked to be busy. She sent Bessie home but neither Joe nor Whistler would leave her.

'We promised the master we'd stay and look after you.'

'I'm perfectly capable of looking after myself,' Charity told them but with a smile because she was grateful for their concern and their loyalty.

'I tell you what,' she said with a look of mischief about her, 'there is a special errand I need you both to go on.'

'I really don't think it's a good idea for us to go and fetch Moses. He needs a bit of time to lick his wounds. He may not have chosen his bride but it hurts a man when she chooses someone else.'

'Actually, my errand had nothing to do with Moses. I hate the thought of him being hurt and alone but I know you are right and,' she paused, 'I admire Molly for marrying for love and not because it suits her family.

'They had ideas of merging East Park Farm with their own - and who can blame them, but maybe it will all work out in the end.'

'So, miss,' Joe said, 'what was it you want us to do?'

'It's a bit of undercover detective work,' Charity told them. 'You remember you told me about the man who was robbed of his gold watch?'

The lads nodded.

'I know nothing about the customers at the Bowl and Pin. I can't go and ask more questions because I've already introduced myself to their landlord and asked him what he knew but . . . we could dress you up in Father's clothes and you could go and see what you can find out.'

The boys didn't take much persuading although they weren't sure the master would be happy about them wearing his clothes.

'Well, don't you both look smart young gentlemen?' Charity said when they appeared some time later. She straightened Whistler's collar.

'Why, thenk you, ma'am,' he said in such a refined voice they all fell about laughing.

Charity furnished them with a little money for ale and helped them make up a simple story as to who they were.

'And remember you're just passing through, so don't be too long,' she called as they wandered down the street into Twyford.

Charity swept the floor and rinsed out the jugs. She was just thinking about locking up when Joe and Whistler returned. They entered the inn from the street and walked up to the bar showing great confidence. For a moment Charity didn't even recognise the two of them.

'Oh, it's you.' She laughed. 'Well, if you can fool me, you'll have done a good job at the Bowl and Pin.'

She poured them all some ale and they sat in the warm kitchen as she listened to what they had to tell.

Moses to the Rescue

'We'd only been in there a few minutes,' Whistler began.

'I'd taken one sip,' Joe added, 'when we were approached by two men. They looked shady characters to me if ever you saw them.'

'They wanted to know if we were travelling far and if we needed protection.'

'Protection?' Charity asked.

'Like an armed escort,' Joe explained. 'They were quite disappointed when we said we had more or less reached the end of our journey which had been uneventful.'

'He told us of the man who'd been robbed, but he said he had rings taken and gold chains — even his boots!'

Charity smiled. She'd often heard stories grow into different ones as the evening wore on and more beer was consumed.

'Would you recognise the men who

approached you?' she asked.

'I think so, although it was dark in there.' 'Were there many customers?' she asked, always eager to know how the other inns compared with the New Bell.

'Dead as a dormouse,' Joe told her and then giggled. 'But they did have the sweetest little maid out the back.' 'Hurry now,' Charity told them, 'put those clothes back in his chest and make sure he'll never know they were touched, let alone borrowed.'

'Here,' Joe said, offering some coppers, 'your change.'

'I think you and Whistler have earned that tonight, don't you?'

'It were fun, miss.'

'Good, and remember, not a word to anyone.'

Charity checked the doors were bolted and poked at the fire. She wasn't sure she had learned anything new this evening but it had been fun and had passed the time.

★ ★ ★

Her father returned the following day feeling tired and sore from the travelling. 'Hope is to marry Rev Mason at mid-summer.'

'Can you really see Hope as a vicar's wife?' Charity asked her father.

'I'm not sure. It was a surprise to me but he seems a very pleasant chap and already fond of our Hope. I think she will happily adapt to her new role. He certainly seemed a decent sort with many ideas of his own. I hope that won't get him into trouble.'

'It wouldn't have suited Faith, being a vicar's wife.'

'No, she's not cut out to that simple sort of life.'

'Did you get to see her?' Charity asked. 'Alas, no, but I hear from Hope that she is enjoying married life and has become great friends with Sir John's wife, of all people.' 'The Sir John who hopes to move here?'

'The very same.'

'Well, that could be to our advantage if she behaves herself.'

Peter Bell gave his youngest daughter a questioning look but didn't question her further.

* * *

That evening there was a great storm. The rain fell like iron rods and the wind blew as though it were the end of the world.

Thunder filled the air and the lightning lit up the sky dramatically.

Charity had been born in a thunder storm and always loved to watch them whereas neither of her sisters liked them at all. They always cowered in the background while Charity stood at the window and gave them a running commentary of what was going on outside.

The storm raged on all night. Charity was amazed she managed to get any sleep at all but somehow she did and woke refreshed. The air seemed fresh and clear after the heaviness of the storm.

The stream was higher than usual and everything in the yard had been blown about. There were twigs and leaves everywhere but these could be collected up and used as tinder. Some of her herbs had been damaged but soon she had everything back in order.

Once Charity had put everything in its rightful place she went into the inn to see if her father needed any assistance. He was talking quietly with Moses at the bar.

Charity tried to keep herself busy but she kept being drawn back to Moses. It was as if she was looking at him to see if there was anything different about him but he just seemed the same old Moses she had known most of her life.

Just then Luke the post boy arrived. He told them that the massive oak that stood by the ford had been struck by lightning the previous night and a huge branch had fallen into the river. Furthermore two other trees had been uprooted and were also in the river blocking the ford and making it difficult for carts to cross.

'It's all hands on deck. It'll take many

men to move them, but free firewood if we do.'

Moses and Peter Bell didn't need to be asked twice. They were always ready to go and help out when something like this happened. Leaving Charity in charge once again they hurried off to help clear the ford.

The hours passed before Moses returned and then he came back alone.

'Where's Father?' she asked.

'I think you better come with me,' Moses told her. 'I've borrowed a horse. I'll take you there now.'

Fearing the worst, Charity held on to Moses as he rode her down the country lanes to the ford which divided Moses's farm and the hamlet of Hurst.

There was a hive of activity around the ford. The trees had now been removed and were being chopped up and divided equally between all the helpers. Dog carts were being used to deliver the wood wherever it was needed.

Peter Bell had been taken to one of the nearby hostelries. Charity was shocked to see how pale he looked.

'What happened?' she asked as she went to hold his hand. He was too weak to speak but the landlord explained that he had exhausted himself moving the tree trunks.

'He was tired already from a day's travelling,' Charity told him.

'I've said he's welcome to stay and rest but Moses thought we ought to fetch you.'

As much as Charity wanted to scoop up her father and take him back home so she could nurse him back to health, she could tell just by looking at him that he was too weak to go anywhere.

It was decided that he would stay in Hurst until he was recovered enough to travel home and then Moses would bring him back to the inn.

Moses knew the landlord well as his farmland was close by. Charity made her father comfortable and thanked the landlord for his kindness. They insisted she stayed and shared a meal with them.

As Charity ate the bread and cheese

she was offered she listened to the conversations going on around her. She was interested to hear that a local landowner had some time ago had a gold watch and chain stolen but just recently it had turned up.

The man who'd supposedly 'found' it said he was coming to claim his reward. The landowner made sure he was given a good meal and a decent pair of boots but then sent him packing.

Once they had finished eating, Moses offered to take Charity back to the inn.

'Oh, heavens!' she exclaimed. 'I've just left poor Bessie to cope.'

'Those lads of yours will make sure she's fine. They're like family to you and won't let you down.'

'Yes, Moses, that's true. I am very lucky to have so many loyal friends around me.'

There was a pause. Charity looked up into Moses' face wondering if he would say that he, too, was a loyal friend. Instead he met her eyes and then smiled briefly before turning away.

She had no idea how he was feeling. She had told herself a thousand times that the marriage between Moses and Molly had been an arranged marriage for the convenience of both families rather than a love match, but still didn't really know how Moses had ever felt - about her or about Molly for that matter.

She needed to hear of his feelings from his own lips. She suspected he only loved her as a sister but they had never shared any conversations about their feelings for one another. They were just two young people who'd grown up together.

On the journey back home, now that she knew her father was in safe hands, Charity was more aware of the strong man who cradled her in front of him as he rode them back to the inn. Charity decided she liked the feeling of his arms around her but all too soon the journey was over and Moses helped her down and back into the New Bell.

As always he was the perfect gentleman. Charity had no cause to complain, although tonight, having felt his arms around her, she realised she longed to be kissed by him.

Instead she had to content herself with taking her time checking how the burns on Moses's arm were doing.

'Well done, you've kept it clean and it's not become infected.'

'That's all thanks to you,' he told her.

Moses stayed to help while the inn was busy but once it quietened down he returned to his farm.

Joe and Whistler had barrels to go and collect and full ones to deliver.

'If you happen to see Constable Hargreaves on your travels, can you tell him I have a jug of ale waiting for him?'

'I hope you're not offering him a bribe,' Joe said in mock horror for everyone knew that Charity would never stoop so low and that Constable Hargreaves knew he was so well respected and fair that no-one would dare to offer him money.

Once a stranger tried to bribe him and was put in the stocks. It had been a lesson to them all.

One Mystery Solved

Later that afternoon Constable Hargreaves appeared at the kitchen door.

'I hear your father's been taken ill,' he said. 'How is he?'

'Hopefully it's nothing that a good rest won't cure, but he's spending a few days with the landlord in Hurst until he's strong enough to make it back here.'

'And you'll be all right on your own?' The constable seemed concerned. He'd known her and the Bell family all her life and in many ways he was like a second father figure.

'I'll be fine and besides, I'm not on my own. Bessie, Joe and Whistler are always here with me and Moses has been calling in.'

Charity felt herself blush, so she turned to set the kettle on the fire.

'You remember the incident of the man who claimed to be robbed by a highwayman and who said he had a gold watch stolen?'

The constable nodded.

'When I asked at the Bowl and Pin the landlord told me he'd been drinking in there and had carelessly shown his gold watch to anyone who wanted to see it. The landlord remembered some initials on it and it seems this same watch, and possibly the same man who acquired it has now returned it to its rightful owner, a landowner in Hurst. But he didn't get the reward he was after, just a good meal and a pair of boots.'

The constable stroked his chin as he took it all in.

'Are you suggesting he stole the watch in the first place?'

'He may have done, or perhaps he really did happen upon it in the bushes where someone else had hidden it.

'Anyway, this same man and a friend took to offering to protect others from the so-called highwayman. They were earning quite a bit of money escorting women up to the road or into the village.'

'Do you think it was a hoax and there

never was a highwayman in the first place?'

'Exactly so,' Charity told him. 'I only wish that were the case with Sir John, but he was genuinely held up and robbed.'

'Nonetheless,' Constable Hargreaves said, 'I shall make it known to Sir John that this report of another highwayman was fraudulent. I think it might help him reconsider his decision to move elsewhere.'

'I was hoping you'd say that,' Charity said. 'Oh, and I've got something else to show you.'

She went to the dresser and retrieved Joe's sketch of the man they'd been watching in the bar.

'I can't swear he is a criminal,' Charity said, 'but he sat in the bar nursing one drink all evening just watching and listening. We all agreed he looked suspicious but maybe he was an innocent stranger.'

She showed Constable Hargreaves the sketch and he stroked his chin.

'It's a good likeness,' Charity told him.

'Joe's got a real talent for drawing, not that he has much call for it in the stables.'

'Keep this safe,' Hargreaves said. 'As you say, we can't condemn a man for sitting alone with a drink, but I'll know the face if I see it again.'

'Should I show the other publicans?' Charity asked. 'I mean, if I were collecting local information, I'd try different inns so I didn't draw attention to myself and perhaps I might hear other tales in another establishment.'

Constable Hargreaves gave Charity a long stare.

'Good thinking,' he said at last. 'Sometimes it's wise to try to think like one of them, although sometimes I wonder what goes through their minds.'

'I'll take his picture into the Dog and to

Widow Baldwin on the corner and then if the lads are delivering or collecting barrels, I may get them to take it with them, but I'll make sure they keep it safe. It could prove to be important.'

'Good work again, lass,' the constable told her. 'Now where was that ale you promised me?'

* * *

Sir John was relieved that his attack seemed to be an isolated unusual occurrence and not the normal course of events in Twyford. With this in mind he decided he would continue as he'd planned and move his family to Twyford, much to the relief of everyone.

He had already bought the house and had plans to extend it. His wife and their daughters had not yet seen the area which was to become their new home and so he arranged for them to come and view the place, although they were not going to move in until it had been made ready for them.

Charity was delighted by the news and even more thrilled when she learned that both her sisters had been invited to join Sir John and his family on their visit to Twyford.

It didn't take long for the good news to travel around the village and before the week was out Sir John had sent various members of his staff to clean and prepare the new manor as best they could for the family to visit.

This inevitably meant local girls were employed to help with the cleaning and cooking. A team of groundsmen and gardeners were busy making the landscape look neat and tidy once more.

Sir John himself was the first to arrive. He had many plans for the old manor and was keen to implement them. On his arrival he had more plans drawn up to adapt the house to suit him and his extended family.

Once again there was a wave of optimism throughout Twyford and it was contagious. Fortunately Peter Bell was now rested and, with Moses's help, he arrived back at the New Bell.

Charity exchanged looks with Bessie as soon as they saw him. He looked so pale and had lost weight.

'He's aged twenty years!' Bessie said.

'He's become an old man.'

'Shh,' Charity whispered, 'don't let him hear you say that. It'll be our job to feed him up and nurse him back to health.'

Business picked up again at the New Bell which was a relief to Charity although she was beginning to wonder if they would have to employ more help if her father wasn't able to pull his weight.

However, even though Peter Bell looked weak, he was in good spirits and was keen to keep himself busy even if it was Charity who did most of the running around.

Once the midday rush had died down, Peter Bell retired to his bed for a nap. He was easily exhausted these days but the short sleep did him good.

Charity began to clear up but then remembered the sketch she had hidden in the dresser.

'Bessie, I'm just visiting the Dog and then Widow Baldwin. I won't be too long.'

Big Tom was eating some broth in the

kitchen area of the Dog. Charity showed him the sketch.

'I'm not saying this man has done any harm, but something about him made me suspicious. Have you seen him?'

'I'm sure he was in last night. Quiet fellow, sat in the corner. He gave me no trouble and in my book that's no cause for concern.'

'Of course he may be totally innocent but on the other hand he may be a scout on the look-out for news of someone carrying something precious and worth stealing.' 'Is that what you think he was up to?' Big Tom asked.

'I'm just being cautious and asking around. I have nothing against the man.'

'Does Hargreaves know you're after his job?' Big Tom laughed.

Charity laughed with him and headed toward the Bell on the corner of the crossroads.

Inside she found Widow Baldwin directing her workers. She looked surprised to see Charity as their paths rarely crossed.

'And what business do you have here, Miss Bell?' the older woman asked.

Charity showed her Joe's sketch.

'This man has been acting suspiciously. He hasn't actually done anything wrong, to my knowledge, but I was just wondering if he'd been in your inn?'

Widow Baldwin barely glanced at the picture and shook her head but one of her lads looked at the picture.

'I've seen him,' the man said. 'Codger, I think they call him. I was passing the Bowl and Pin and it looked to me as though he'd been thrown out of there. Why do you ask?'

Widow Baldwin now took the picture from Charity and had a proper look at it.

'I don't know if you'd heard that some men were saying they'd been robbed by a highwayman and a gold watch had been stolen?'

Everyone nodded. It was rare that news like that would stay a secret for long in a village like Twyford where everybody knew everyone else and their business.

'Well, it appears it was all an elaborate

hoax. I'm not sure of all the details but I think either Codger or someone found or stole a gold watch, then dressed as a gentleman and pretended he'd had it stolen from him.

'Then he, or one of his accomplices, approached the owner of the gold watch saying he'd found it and he wanted a reward. He got a good meal and a pair of boots for his trouble.

'But that's not the end of the story, having put the fear of highwaymen into people's minds, they then started to offer a service of protecting travellers, especially vulnerable women and children from robbers who didn't exist in the first place.'

'Well I never,' the man said. He actually sounded quite impressed by the scam.

'There's nothing new in that,' Widow Baldwin told them. 'I remember my father, or perhaps my grandfather, telling me of Thomas Chandler, it must have been the late seventeen-forties.

'He claimed he'd been robbed of bank

notes between Hare Hatch and Twyford. They were worth about one thousand pounds and a silver watch!'

Everyone gasped. It was a huge amount of money.

'Mr Chandler claimed against Sonning parish and was awarded about a thousand pounds in damages. However, there was a lawyer called Edward Wise — I always remember his name because it seemed so apt — he was able to prove it was all false and Mr Chandler was sentenced to seven years' transportation! So, let that be a lesson to you all.'

'I do vaguely remember that story,' Charity said. 'I can't have been very old but it involved such a lot of money, I recall people talking about it.'

'You ask Constable Hargreaves, he'll remember it. It may even have been Mr Wise who got him to become a constable in the first place.'

'So, what shall we do if we see this man?' Widow Baldwin asked. Her manner was much more amenable now, Charity noticed. 'Shall I let you know?'

'Please do,' Charity told her. 'As I said, he may be innocent but it looked to me as though he was busy listening to everyone else's conversation and watching for someone flashing a bit of cash about. You know the sort. He just looked up to no good.'

'As a landlady, you do get to know who's good and who's not,' Widow Baldwin agreed, treating Charity as an equal for the first time. 'I think it's good we share information like this. We all ought to work together more.'

'I certainly agree,' Charity said, smiling at the older woman.

She left the Bell and wondered how long she'd been out. She calculated there was still time for her to see Constable Hargreaves if she were quick, and still get back to help Bessie.

'Ah, yes,' Hargreaves said, 'I do remember the Chandler case. You'd have only been about six when it happened.

What a clever scoundrel he was, although not clever enough!'

'Our suspicious man, the one in the

sketch, has been identified as Codger.'

'Good work,' Hargreaves told her. 'I'll keep an eye open for him. In fact, I may go and see the landlord of the Bowl and Pin again and see if he can fill in the gaps we have in this story — how Codger is involved, or whether we are looking at two different cases.'

'I must be off, I've left poor Bessie with loads to do.'

'How's your father?' the constable asked. 'He's improving, although he does get

tired. He was having a nap when I left so I had better get home.'

* * *

News reached them of Sir John's family arriving in a convoy of two carriages that day, followed by more later. Charity wondered if that had included her sisters. She hoped she would have the opportunity to see them while they were staying so close by but with the extra work at the

142

inn, she didn't know if she'd be able to get away.

She also didn't know if she would actually be invited, as she had no appropriate clothes to wear, and she knew how important it was not to let her sisters down in public. They were living such a different life to hers now.

One afternoon, in the lull between the end of the lunchtime rush and before the evening, she was surprised and delighted to hear a carriage pull up outside and two finely dressed young ladies alight.

'Faith! Hope!' she called and threw her arms around them.

'Lady Mary wants to meet you,' Hope told her younger sister. 'She thinks Faith and I look so alike we could be twins and she wonders if you will also look like a pea from the same pod.'

'I'd be honoured,' Charity replied cautiously but she had no need to worry because instantly Hope produced a box from the carriage and inside was a beautiful gown.

'It's only an old thing,' Faith told her,

'but it should fit you and once you've been presented to Lady Mary we will show you around.'

'I hope Father will be able to spare me,' Charity said almost to herself. 'It's been very busy and, he's not been well.'

The girls went to see their father but they didn't stay long. It was agreed that Charity would visit the following afternoon and that a carriage would be sent to collect her.

'There's no need, I could walk,' Charity told them.

'Nonsense, that's not the sort of entrance you should make. And besides, if you walked your gown and shoes will be ruined, to say nothing of your hair. You must make yourself presentable.'

Charity looked at Faith and then at Hope and her heart sank.

'I hope you are not trying to match me up with some awful suitor.'

'The only way for a woman to make something of her life is to marry well,' Faith told her and Hope nodded.

Charity knew they had her best interests at heart and maybe she would be able to do more good if she married well and had even a small disposable income. But her husband might wish to live elsewhere and he might not approve of her visiting the poor or helping the disadvantaged.

At least now her father didn't comment on her comings and goings and never admonished her if she took food to the poor or housed a beggar.

'We will see you tomorrow,' Faith said as she got back into the carriage. Charity couldn't help thinking she seemed rather aloof. Hope kissed her cheek and then climbed into the carriage for their return journey.

Charity walked round to the far side of the carriage in order to say a proper farewell to Faith but she was sitting back and almost hidden in the shadows.

'See you tomorrow, although I don't think you'll recognise me in my new gown. Thank you so much.'

She waved until the carriage was out of sight and then caught a glimpse of

Bessie watching them disappear.

'I suppose we had better get back to work,' Charity said with a smile.

She knew Bessie was disappointed that neither of her sisters had acknowledged their loyal servant who had been with them for years.

'I'm hoping you'll be able to help me with my hair,' Charity told her.

'I'm no lady's maid,' Bessie said, 'but one of my sisters is, so I'll visit her. She'll tell me what to do. I won't let you down, miss.'

'Thank you, Bessie, I don't know what I'd do without you.'

As Charity busied herself preparing a rabbit stew she thought about her sisters. They had both changed into fine young women and already seemed so distant.

Charity would have liked to walk in the meadows with them, paddle in St Patrick's stream and make daisy-chains, but she guessed that it would now be deemed as unladylike to do such simple and innocent things.

Charity peeled and chopped more

potatoes. Faith had seemed unusually quiet and reserved, but at least she had made the effort to come and visit, and they had brought her a dress and slippers to wear so that she could come and meet Lady Mary and to be shown around the manor.

Charity was looking forward to her visit and worked especially hard that evening to make sure she could be spared for a couple of hours the following afternoon.

Just as she finished chopping carrots she looked up at the sound of a familiar laugh.

'Moses, I was just thinking about you and wondering how your arm was healing.'

Moses rolled up his sleeve to show her that his arm, although still red, was mending well.

'I was lucky,' he told her. 'Fortunate not to have been more seriously hurt and lucky to have you to look after me. Not everyone would have known what to do.'

'I'm just glad it has worked.'

Bessie fetched Moses a drink and he

sat at the table while Charity worked. She told him about the visit from her sisters and her invitation to meet Sir John's wife.

'Is your sister all right now?' Moses asked. Charity stopped what she was doing and looked at him.

'Which one?' she asked.

'Faith. I saw her in the village outside the milliner's. She was pointing out a bonnet in the shop window. She wasn't wearing a hat herself at the time and I could see her face was marked.'

'Really?' Charity was surprised by all this, not least at how observant Moses was turning out to be. His comment triggered a little memory. Hadn't someone recently mentioned the need for cobwebs to help heal a wound?

Visiting the Manor

The following afternoon Bessie helped Charity get ready for her trip to the manor. Both girls were excited about the prospect of trying on the beautiful pale blue gown that Hope had given her.

'Is it silk, miss?' Bessie asked.

'I'm no expert,' Charity told her, 'but I think it probably is. I've certainly never had a dress so beautiful, except perhaps the one I borrowed for Faith's wedding.'

This one was long and full with a rounded scooped neck. Then she wore a pink silk sash and a matching pink rose, also made of silk. Her slippers were of the same pale blue material as the dress and wearing them made Charity feel light and dainty, as though she could dance and dance.

'It's so beautiful, miss,' Bessie said for the third time.

'It is lovely but I can't imagine wearing something like this all the time.

Think how long it's taken us to get ready! Think of all the things we could have been doing.'

'You work so hard, miss,' Bessie reminded her. 'It will do you good to dress up and pretend to be a proper lady for the day.'

'That's exactly how I feel.' Charity laughed. 'As though it is all a pretence, which it is, because I don't belong in the manor with the likes of Sir John and Lady Mary, or even to be seated alongside my hoity-toity sisters.'

'They are like strangers now, miss,' Bessie said sadly. 'I can't see you going down that road. At least I hope not.'

'This is my home,' Charity told her firmly, 'and Father, you, Joe and Whistler are my family.'

Charity's father looked in disbelief when his youngest daughter came downstairs.

'How did I ever manage to get three such beautiful girls? I thought you were a real lady when I first caught a glimpse of you. I guessed you must have lost your way and wandered down here.'

It had taken Bessie longer than intended for her to do Charity's hair and so they were just about ready when the carriage arrived to collect her. She was disappointed that both her sisters hadn't come to escort her, but Hope was there looking confident in all her finery.

'I knew that dress would look gorgeous on you. It was one of Faith's but she's grown tired of it and her husband has bought her several new gowns so you may as well keep it.'

'That's so generous,' Charity told her, although she was already wondering when she would ever get a chance to wear it again.

As the carriage took them back through the village, Hope asked the driver to go slowly so they could savour the sights, as if she knew how much Charity wished to be seen riding through Twyford in a black covered carriage like a lady.

'I always think it's interesting to see familiar places from a carriage window, they always look so different.'

'They do, don't they?' Charity agreed with her sister as she waved at Constable Hargreaves standing outside the Dog speaking with Big Tom.

A little further on they passed the milliner's where Hope had started work as an apprentice some time ago.

'Do you miss working there?'

'No, I do not!' Hope laughed. 'Of course I'd much rather have the life I live now. It was hard work in that shop. My fingers were always sore and people were rude to me, always ordering me about.'

'I hope you remember that now, and treat your servants kindly,' Charity told her. 'I hope Faith remembers her roots, too.'

'I do try,' Hope told her honestly, 'but some of these girls are very simple.'

Charity bit her lip. She thought of Bessie. Over the years she had learned that the best way to get the most out of Bessie was to give her one instruction at a time so as not to confuse her and to praise her whenever she did something well. So far it had worked and Bessie was now a loyal servant and more able than she used to be.

'I always buy my hats from Mistress Brown,' Hope reassured her sister. 'In fact, I was encouraging Sir John's wife and daughters to open an account with her.'

'Moses said he saw Faith going in there the other day.'

Hope gave a little cough.

'That didn't go well, unfortunately. Feathers are all the rage but Faith wanted something with a little net veil. There was one in the window but Mistress Brown was very reluctant to sell it to her, but as usual Faith managed to get her way even though her maid nearly had a fit when she saw it.'

'Why? Faith has such good taste.' 'The hat is lovely but it's last season's design and it doesn't work with the way Faith has her hair at the moment. The two of them were arguing as to how they could make it work. Of course, Faith got her way as usual.'

Something made Charity feel uncomfortable about the reason why her eldest sister would insist on wearing a bonnet with a net even if the milliner and her maidservant told her it was not the height of fashion. It was so unlike Faith, although she was strong minded and could certainly be stubborn.

'Well, at least she is using local tradespeople and she is to be commended for that. It's what Twyford needs. It's been so hard here due to the years of wet summers and failed crops, but things are looking up now.'

'You are so loyal to this place, aren't you?' Hope said and looked straight at Charity, their hazel eyes meeting. 'When you have travelled as much as I have you'll realise there are much prettier places.'

'Hope!' Charity gasped at her sister. 'I can't believe you would ever say such a thing. Twyford is home and always will be. It's the most wonderful place on God's earth.'

'If you say so,' Hope said with a little smile.

Charity was amazed by the beautiful detail and rich material of the crimson dress worn by Sir John's wife, Lady Mary. He, too, looked very grand in his smart coat and collar. It was as if she had entered a whole new world.

Sir John's children were delightful. He had three little girls and they reminded Charity of herself and her sisters. The only difference was that his girls were all dainty and ladylike - unlike the Bell girls who ran in the fields and climbed trees.

'And how are you progressing in your efforts to catch the highwayman?' Sir John asked her quietly while his wife was attending to the children. Charity could feel herself blush.

'I can say for sure that it was not Mr Turpin,' she began.

Sir John almost looked disappointed and she had heard someone say that rich people sometimes felt that if they had to be robbed, they would rather a notorious villain did the deed, than some ragamuffin no-one had heard of.

'Of course he could have had an

155

apprentice,' she added quickly to make him feel better. 'I have visited the Thicket, where the attack took place and I have heard several eye witness statements, although not everyone agrees whether it was a lone rider or a small group. What did you think?'

Sir John was about to answer when a lively puppy ran up to him and distracted his attention.

Tea was then served and the opportunity to question Sir John was lost, at least for the time being.

Both Faith and Hope had gone through the rules of what to do and what not to do during her visit. Charity was so anxious not to get it wrong that she became quiet and reserved, hardly saying a word.

Thankfully Sir John's delightful daughters were eager to play with a new puppy and made rather a lot of noise. Before long Sir John declared he had had enough and sent the girls outside into the garden with the dog accompanied by Hope, who had been allowed to show Charity around.

Hope was keen to show her sister the best rooms in the place but Charity was insistent on seeing the kitchen.

She had more than one reason for this. For a start she wanted to be able to compare it with her own kitchen at the New Bell, although she guessed there might not be much of a comparison, and she also wanted to meet the cook.

'I don't think that's what Sir John had in mind when he agreed for me to show you around his new home.'

'Oh, please,' Charity begged. Hope didn't actually agree but she did lead her sister down a stone staircase to the kitchens below.

Charity was amazed at the size of the kitchen. She knew it was going to be a large room but even the pantry was almost as large as her kitchen. She chatted to the cook and complimented her on the game pie that was ready on the large wooden table.

Charity realised she felt more at ease chatting with the servants than she had with Sir John and his family. However, the cook was clearly on her best behaviour and not used to having someone she considered a lady asking her about her cookery skills.

'I did enjoy those biscuits you served us. I don't suppose I could have some to take back to my father and our servants?'

'Certainly, miss,' the cook said and went to fetch a few of her home-made biscuits, carefully wrapping them in muslin for Charity to take with her. 'I'll have George put them in the carriage for you.'

'That's very kind, thank you. I'm sure they'll appreciate that.'

'I'm sure they will,' the cook said, clearly impressed that Charity would think of her father and her servants and treat them well.

'Shall we venture up the stairs now?' Hope asked, a little impatiently.

'Thank you so much for showing me your kitchen. I'm impressed by the way you keep it. Sir John is very lucky to have you.'

She then followed Hope back up the stairs in order to see the rest of the house. Faith remained with Sir John and his wife. They had become firm friends.

The manor was still under wraps for the most part as it had been unlived in for several years before Sir John acquired it and even now only a few rooms had been made habitable for the family to live in during their short visit.

'But oh, they have such grand plans for the place,' Hope was telling her as they entered a smaller room where she and Faith were sleeping during their stay.

Hope immediately went to check on her complexion in the looking-glass near the window. Meanwhile Charity wandered around the room touching the smooth surface of the dressing table and sitting down to feel how soft the bed was.

As she was admiring the surroundings, Charity noticed a piece of paper. It was a receipt for a hat but the name of the proprietor was not Mistress Brown but someone else. Clearly Hope was not always so loyal to her previous employer.

On closer inspection, Charity realised it was not in Hope's name but Faith's and she felt instantly guilty for having judged Hope so badly. The receipt intrigued her because the proprietor was from St James's Street in London and appeared to be from a married couple. He was a hatter for gentlemen and she was a milliner making hats for ladies, even some royals.

'I wonder if King George gets his hats from here?' she said aloud.

'Have you heard about his new bride?' Hope asked, suddenly sounding excited. 'Her name is Princess Charlotte and she's from Germany. They are due to be married in the autumn as soon as she arrives in England. I wish I could go.'

'You'd never be invited to a royal wedding!' Charity laughed at her sister.

'No, I know, but you can always dream.' Hope looked wistfully outside, staring into the distance.

Charity took one final glance at the receipt and to her surprise she saw it was for a tri-cornered hat.

'Are you all right?' Hope asked as Charity sank back down on to the bed. 'You've suddenly gone very pale.'

More Disturbing News

Charity felt better once she was outside in the fresh air in the beautifully land-scaped gardens. Unfortunately she still felt a little dizzy due to all the thoughts going on inside her head.

'How are you getting on with our brother-in-law James?' Charity asked. 'Tell me, what's he like?'

'He always seems most charming,' Hope told her. 'Faith says she has no complaints and he certainly adores her. He is the most generous of husbands.'

'Does he have any brothers?' Charity asked and much to her surprise Hope clapped her hands.

'At last!' she said. 'I was wondering if you would ever show any interest in joining us here but alas both his brothers are already married and one lives abroad in some God-forsaken place that is too hot to mention. He hasn't been seen in years.'

'What about a cousin?' Charity continued, much to her sister's delight.

'No, I don't believe he has.' 'What about his other brother?'

'I told you they're both married and the one who lives here is weak. The poor man walks with a limp. He wouldn't be able to keep up with you even if he were free to wed, if that's what you're thinking.'

Charity let her sister continue to think what she wanted about why she had suddenly shown an interest in her brother- in-law and his family.

'I really think I ought to be going home,' Charity said and the carriage was called.

'Shall I accompany you?' Hope offered although Charity could see she would be happier to remain at the manor.

'Thank you, but I will be fine. Please thank Sir John and his wife for their hospitality and give my love to Faith. I was sorry not to see more of her. Oh, and thank the cook for the biscuits. Bessie and the boys will love them.'

Charity kissed her sister goodbye and entered the carriage. It was not a long journey but, because of the state of the roadways the driver had been asked to take it slowly and carefully.

On the way Charity had been so keen to take in every single detail, no matter how small or seemingly insignificant. However, on the way back she hardly noticed a thing, she was so deep in thought.

She thought back to her sisters and how close they had all been when they were young, and yet now both Faith and Hope seemed so distant and aloof. It was true they were now living a very different life but Charity couldn't understand why they had changed so much. She was sure that even if she had lots of money and lived in a fine house, she would not forget her roots or the people she had grown up with.

All Faith could think about, Charity was sure, was how she looked in the eyes of others. Not that it would bother Faith at all that her own sister wasn't impressed with her behaviour. She only wanted to impress those that mattered and sadly it didn't seem that Charity was among that number.

Hope had changed, too, but at least she was civil to her little sister. Sadly, Charity could see Hope ending up like Faith and in the not-too-distant future. They had risen too high in society to want to admit to having a pub landlord in their family.

Charity blushed again as she remembered Sir John asking how close she was to catching the culprit who'd robbed him. At least he knew who she was, but was she going to have to break some unpleasant news to him? Would she be praised for her honesty or shunned for slander?

To Charity's relief, Moses was waiting for her when she arrived back home and he'd already been to the water pump and saved her a journey.

He bowed to her like a gentleman as he helped her step down from the carriage. He held her hand and made her turn around to show him her gown.

'You'll have to excuse me a moment,' Charity told him. 'I need to get out of these clothes and into my old things. They are much more comfortable.'

She handed Bessie the biscuits she'd bought back with her.

'There should be enough for us all. Moses can have mine as I had one at the manor.

They are delicious. You should have seen the size of their kitchen and all the equipment they had. You wouldn't believe it.'

'I'll put the kettle on, miss,' Bessie said. 'You go and change back into our Miss Charity.'

'So, tell me all about it. How are your sisters?' Moses asked once Charity returned a little while later.

'They are well. Sir John was kind. He has grand plans for the manor and in time it will be a sight for sore eyes.'

'But?' Moses asked. 'I gather your visit wasn't all rosy?'

Charity looked around her but Bessie

was busy elsewhere making sure Joe and Whistler had their biscuits and her father was asleep in the corner. She leaned forward and whispered.

'Moses, you're never going to believe this, but I think I've discovered who the mystery highwayman is and if I disclose his identity I suspect it will cause more harm than good.'

'You're not going to tell me that Sir John made it all up or paid someone to pretend to rob him so he could claim sympathy or insurance like that Chandler chap?'

'No, although that would be bad enough.'

'So, are you going to tell me more?' he asked. 'A problem shared is a problem halved, and you know I will keep it a secret if you decide not to name the culprit.'

Until then, Charity had intended to keep her thoughts to herself until she had had time to consider them fully but here was a chance to share her worries and her feelings. Moses knew the people she

would implicate and he was wise enough
to help her come to the right decision.

Naming Names

Charity lowered her voice so that only Moses could hear.

'I think the highwayman was James, my brother-in-law, Faith's husband.'

Moses considered her statement for a moment or two and then leant forward, keeping his voice just above a whisper.

'And what makes you come to that conclusion?'

'In Faith's room she was in possession of a receipt from a London Hatters for a tri- cornered hat just like the one the highwayman wore!'

'Owning a hat does not make you a highwayman.' Moses laughed.

'There's more,' Charity told him. She was glad to be able to put her thoughts into order. 'On both occasions, James had the opportunity to carry out the crimes.

'He was coming to visit Faith when Sir John was robbed and on the eve of his wedding he was in the vicinity when the Dowager was held up . . . and I found a signet ring which could be the one that belonged to Sir John. It was hidden in a drawer in Faith's room. She must know and be covering for him.'

Again Moses listened and thought about what she had said before he responded.

'I am sure many wealthy men own those particular hats and signet rings and may well have been around at the time of both crimes. I think you need more evidence before you accuse anyone.'

'Now that I've said it aloud to you,' Charity admitted, 'it does sound a bit feeble. But I was so sure. I even asked Hope if he had any brothers who might be taken for him as I hated the thought of accusing my own brother-in-law and what that would do to Faith.'

'And does he have a brother who he could be protecting?'

'He has two but one lives abroad and didn't even come home for the wedding and his other brother is weak and limps.

I don't believe he is able to ride a horse, so that rather rules him out.'

'I think we also have to think about motive,' Moses told her. 'James is a rich man in his own right. If he was the culprit and found guilty, he would hang. Surely only a desperate man would take the risk?'

'I can't argue with you there,' Charity agreed. 'I am better at proving people innocent rather than finding them guilty.' She laughed. 'Thank you so much for listening to me. I feel much better now, and

I am so glad I didn't jump to conclusions and make a fool of myself.'

★   ★   ★

Charity gathered from several of her customers that there was now a regular guard at Maidenhead Thicket. Someone said he was paid by the village of Littlewick Green and was hired because he was accurate with a gun.

'And is he there every night?' she

asked. 'Every single night from sunset to sunrise,' one of the regulars told her. 'And he's reliable, too. He won't let them down.'

'But one man against a band of high-waymen - does he have any chance?' Charity argued.

'He's built like a haystack,' she was told, 'and I have heard he's set to gain a handsome prize if he catches the rogues.'

'I'm glad to hear it,' Charity told them. She even wondered if Sir John had contributed to the hiring of this giant.

The inn was quiet but it was still early. Charity had wiped down all the tables and was just returning to the kitchen when she saw Bessie looking distressed.

'I thought you'd gone home ages ago.'

'That I did. But I had to come back.'

'Why? Is something the matter?' Charity asked, seeing how deathly pale the girl looked. 'Do you need some ale?'

'I had this vision, clear as day it was,' Bessie began. At this point most people rolled their eyes and walked away. Few people took Bessie seriously because she often had visions or dreams that she couldn't explain.

Charity poured her a drink and bade her sit down. She felt sorry for the girl and always made time to listen to her. In fact, a lot of what Bessie said turned out to be true. The only trouble was when Bessie described something she saw, she didn't always understand what it meant and so didn't always tell the right people or use the correct words.

It was only with hindsight after an event that Charity was reminded of something odd Bessie had said and realised that actually she had known what would happen, or had predicted an outcome.

In fact, looking back she had been adamant from the start that Molly and Moses would never marry. Charity had not taken much notice at all because she assumed Bessie was just trying to make her feel better, but actually Bessie had been right all along.

'Are you feeling better now?' Charity

asked. Bessie had a little colour back in her cheeks.

'I saw you, miss,' she said and her voice wobbled as though something was really troubling her. 'In your hand you had a large forked stick. You had a worried look on your face and you kept turning the stick around as if divining for water.'

'And what do you think it means?' Charity asked.

'It was a bad feeling. Something really dreadful is going to happen and it's going to happen to you.'

This took Charity by surprise but Bessie had spoken her words and Charity had heard them.

★ ★ ★

For the next few days Charity tried to forget Bessie's vision but because it was so vague, she couldn't help thinking about it and trying to decide what it meant.

Charity was not normally a worrier but having heard that something bad was going to happen that would affect her, she was anxious when her father mentioned going to a nearby farm to offer to help with the hay making. Would he be taken ill again?

Instead she persuaded him to go and visit Miss Rose.

'I understand her roses have been wonderful this year and she hopes to make rose water. You remember Mother used to say her rose water was the best she'd ever had?'

'What would she want with me getting in her way?' her father asked.

'I heard she needs someone to help her. At least go over to Hurst and speak with her. I'll come with you. I'd love to see her rose garden. Short Samuel was telling me you smell it before you see it because the roses fill the air.'

At midday Charity was busy serving food to guests when she caught a glimpse of Moses out of the corner of her eye. Once more she was filled with dread. Was something awful going to happen to Moses?

That would be a cruel twist of fate

now that he was no longer betrothed she hoped beyond hope that Moses would notice her.

The day passed uneventfully. That evening Luke called in for ale and a meal and told them the news that another coach had been held up and robbed at Maidenhead Thicket.

'But I thought it was now protected by an armed guard,' Charity questioned. 'What went wrong with the plan?'

'The guard was asleep. They call him the Badger because he sleeps all day and is awake all night. Some say something was put in his drink, a herb to make him sleep, perhaps.'

'Was it the same highwayman?' Charity asked.

'From what I've heard, I'd say it was.' 'So, he's still around despite having an armed guard on duty?'

'He may not be around for much longer because the coachdriver was a cunning man. He attempted to attack the highwayman and pull him from his horse.'

'And was he successful?'

'Alas no, but he did cut a piece of cloth from the cloak worn by the highwayman.'

Charity poured Luke another mug of ale and thanked him for telling his story.

Later that night as she lay on her straw mattress she wondered if this was what was meant by Bessie's prediction. The story was distressing and in some way it could affect them all, but Charity was not at the centre of it and what was meant by the forked stick?

Inspection

In the morning Charity and her father made the journey to Hurst to speak with Miss Rose. Miss Rose was in her fifties, a similar age to her father. She was short and round with yellow curly hair and a cheery face.

She greeted them like old friends despite the fact that they had only met on a handful of occasions.

There were roses everywhere. It was like a forest of rose bushes in the gardens surrounding the house and then other roses climbed up the wall or along the fence. The air was heady with their aroma and almost made you feel drunk with happiness.

'Do you have a favourite?' Charity asked Miss Rose. 'I've always liked the look of this one although it has no scent.'

'I like this one,' Miss Rose pointed to a deep red rose that almost looked like velvet. 'It smells divine.'

Miss Rose had been delighted to become reacquainted with Mr Bell. Over the years she had employed several young girls to help her harvest the rose petals and to turn them into rose water. These girls had grown up and become mothers and had grown in confidence. Occasionally they overstepped the mark and took too many liberties. 'It upset me so much I sent them all away,' Miss Rose told them. 'And now I need help because I can't do it all on my own.'

Charity could see her father look uncomfortable. He obviously didn't see himself as someone who collected in rose petals. That was a job for a lady, not a strong man like himself.

'What I need,' Miss Rose was saying, 'is some help in getting the right young girls to help me here and then, once I've trained them, I need someone to check up on them every so often to make sure they are doing as they are told.

'I can do it most of the time but I find they respond better sometimes to a master rather than a mistress. I'll also need help cutting back the roses on Lady's Day and some fences mending and there are a few things that need fixing around the place.'

Straight away Charity could see her father relax. He was good at fixing things and she knew he could help Miss Rose.

'Miss Baldwin might be able to help with the rosewater,' Charity said. 'I was talking to Widow Baldwin the other day and she told me the girl needed some work.'

'Leave it with me,' Peter Bell told Miss Rose. 'We'll ask in the bar if anyone has a daughter who could help. The only problem is that with the manor being reopened, a lot of the young girls are working there and there are plenty of jobs to be had. But Charity and I will do what we can.'

* * *

The following evening Constable Hargreaves arrived at the New Bell with

180

several men. His men were positioned at each of the doors and no-one was allowed to leave until every man had been questioned and their clothing examined.

They were thorough. Even Peter Bell had to convince Constable Hargreaves that his clothes were all intact. He had to fetch his old trunk of clothes to show he wasn't hiding anything. Charity was relieved he made no mention of these clothes having been borrowed recently.

'What exactly are you looking for?' Charity asked.

'The coach driver had a small knife with which to defend himself if needed. When he tried to pull the highwayman from his horse, he pulled at his cloak and he did manage to cut a bit of the cloth. He made a hole rather like the shape of a diamond and the material was black. It wasn't any old cloak, either,' the Constable told her. 'It had probably been stolen from a gentleman.'

Charity had a troubled night's sleep. She tossed and turned as she pictured the highwayman taking the jewel box from Sir John and frightening the Dowager's horses sending them away and then this most recent attack where she pictured many men in dark cloaks and tri-cornered hats sitting impossibly high up on their mounts looking down at her and laughing …

She yawned as she stirred the porridge oats the following morning and was still tired at midday.

'If we're not too busy,' she told her father, 'I'm going to visit the tollgate family and take them some food. I hear they still haven't got a roof over their head and the storm has caused them further problems.'

'You're a good lass,' her father told her. 'I am only doing what any neighbour would do,' she answered. 'And besides, I need a walk in the fresh air to help me stay awake or I'll be no good at all for you this evening.'

Charity's visit was much appreciated and the fresh air had done her good. However, she felt a strange unease when she returned home to see a carriage draw up beside the inn and her sister Hope alight.

'Is something amiss?' Charity asked.

'It is only that we are about to leave Sir

John's house and Faith and I wanted to see you once more before we return to London.'

'Thank you for coming to say good-bye,' Charity said and looked around for Faith but there was no sign of her.

'We are not leaving until tomorrow.' Hope laughed. 'I have been sent to bring you back to the manor. The cook has made her biscuits especially for you. I think you made a big impression on her and she hasn't stopped singing your praises ever since.'

'Hope! Father and I have the inn to run. I can't just drop everything and come to the manor.'

Hope blushed. It was clear she had not thought things through and if events had gone differently, Hope herself would be serving in the inn.

'At least come in and say goodbye to

Father,' Charity told her. Hope nodded and ventured into the dimly lit kitchen. The fire was ablaze and a stew bubbling away making the room warm. Hope removed her cape and set it on the chair before entering the bar to see her father.

Charity didn't know what possessed her but without a second thought she pounced on the black velvet cape that Hope had been wearing and sure enough near the hem was a small tear in the material. A diamond shaped cut.

She reached for her sharpest knife and swiftly cut the cloak from one end to the other making it a little shorter in length and in doing so destroying the original diamond-shaped hole.

Quickly she threw the remnants on the fire and replaced the cloak on the chair.

Hope didn't stay long. Once more she tried to persuade Charity to come with her to the manor.

'I've already told you I can't,' Charity said as Hope made to leave. 'Is this your cape? It's not one I've seen before.'

'It's Faith's. I borrowed it because I felt a chill.'

'Faith's?' Charity felt the blood drain from her as she reached out for the wall to steady herself.

'What's the matter?' Hope asked, looking around for someone to help.

Charity leant against the wall, checked that no-one was in earshot and pulled her sister close to her.

'Have you heard there was another coach robbed and that a quick-thinking coach driver managed to tear a bit of the highwayman's black cloak?' Charity whispered. 'His knife made the shape of a diamond and I've seen that on your cape.' 'No!' Hope said in surprise and began to look at the torn material. 'Whatever's happened?'

'I had to disguise the hole,' Charity told her. 'Can't you see what this means?'

Hope looked blankly at her sister so Charity was forced to go into more detail than she would have liked.

'I hate to say this, but has Faith turned into a highwayman, or woman? Does she fancy herself as Turpin's apprentice?'

'Good grief! What are you saying?' Hope exclaimed but Charity held her arm as she struggled to move away.

'I'm serious.'

'I remember now,' Hope said, still flushed in the face, 'the footman borrowed her cape.' With that she stepped back from Charity and practically ran to the coach where her driver was waiting for her.

All Charity could do was to watch as her sister disappeared into the distance leaving her with a sinking feeling in the pit of her stomach.

Proving Innocence

For the second night in a row Charity hardly slept at all. She looked wretched in the morning but knew there was no-one she dared confide in. Her worst fears were that Faith would be found guilty of robbery and the sentence would mean she would be hanged. It would make no difference at all to the judge that she was a woman.

Charity now understood Bessie's vision. The forked stick was the dilemma she now faced. Her head told her she should speak to Constable Hargreaves and tell him of all the evidence that pointed to her own sister, but her heart couldn't bring herself to betray her own flesh and blood.

Yet, by concealing the truth, she too was running the risk of having the noose around her own neck or the possibility of being transported.

As dawn approached Charity splashed

water on her face and ran her fingers through her hair. She needed, more than ever, to have her wits about her. She took a few moments to pray for the wisdom to do the right thing, whatever that was.

The day seemed to drag. Charity kept herself busy in order to keep awake. Several times she disappeared to the nearby brook and washed her face in the chilly water. It helped keep her alert.

'Are you poorly, miss?' Bessie asked. 'You don't look right to me.'

'I'm just tired,' Charity told her.

That evening, Moses appeared at the kitchen door with his hat in his hands. Inwardly Charity sighed. What would he think of her now? She had destroyed some evidence and was withholding knowledge from the law that could help apprehend a criminal, except that she couldn't think of her own sister as a wrong-doer.

'What troubles you?' Moses asked. His face was full of concern. 'Can I help?'

Charity longed to be able to confide in Moses. When she had last spoken to him and shared her feelings it had become clear to her what a fool she'd been and perhaps the same would happen again.

However, this time Charity couldn't run the risk of admitting her own worst fears. Perhaps this time she was right.

The more Charity thought about it, the more convinced she was. Faith had always been a tomboy. She loved nothing better than to climb trees, chase the pigs and ride the horses. Out of the three of them she was the one who could ride with most confidence.

Then, of course, Charity thought, there was the scar. The Dowager had managed to scratch the highwayman when she'd been held up. It was clearly no coincidence that Faith had worn a hat with a net to conceal a scar.

Later she had asked her maid for cobwebs which were known to aid healing the skin when it had been cut.

The more she thought about it, the more convinced she was that Faith was guilty.

'What can I do for you, Moses?' she

asked. Her voice sounded as tired and as weary as she felt.

'I was wondering … ' Moses began. 'I thought that perhaps, maybe one day, one day soon, you would come walking with me?'

'Walking? I haven't got time to go walking!' Charity snapped because she was so very tired. 'What is it with everyone?

Firstly Hope thinks I can drop everything and go to the manor and now you think I can leave the New Bell and go for a walk. We have customers to serve and food to prepare.'

Moses shuffled from one foot to another. He hung his head low.

'I didn't necessarily mean now, but maybe one day, perhaps on Sunday after church?' The poor man looked awkward standing there. 'You do know I never loved Molly. I never even got to know if I liked her, nor she me. You know how these things work. You have to do your duty even if it is not your choice.'

The penny dropped and Charity realised, all too late, that her dream of Moses courting her had come at last — only now it was when she didn't deserve such a good man. She herself had become an accessory to a crime.

'Charity!' her father called from the bar. 'Come here!'

Charity did as she was asked and joined her father in the bar. He needed to replace a barrel of beer and there were jugs to be collected.

Fortunately there were not too many men in the inn that evening. Most of them were the usual crowd.

'What's up with you tonight?' one man asked. 'You look like you've got the weight of the world on your shoulders.'

'I'm tired,' Charity told him.

'That's great,' the man said sarcastically. 'I've come here to get away from a moaning wife and all I get is a grumpy barmaid and have to listen to old Isaac moaning about losing his job.' He nodded to the man in the corner drowning his sorrows.

Suddenly Charity felt as though she'd

been slapped around the face. Isaac was Faith's footman. Charity had met him several times. She refilled a jug of ale and took it over to him.

'And what's up with you?' she asked, dreading what she might hear.

'The master accused me of stealing. I ain't done nothing wrong but what can I say?

No-one will believe me. Now I've got no job.'

Charity sat down at the wooden bench with Isaac. She poured them both more ale and fetched a bowl of broth.

'Eat that and then tell me exactly what happened. Exactly,' she said. 'I need to know every detail.'

Isaac finished his broth. It seemed he didn't know what it was he was meant to have stolen. He had been accused and told to leave. He had no right of reply.

'Would it have been the cloak you borrowed?' Charity suggested.

'Come again?'

'My sister, Hope, mentioned you borrowed Faith's cloak. Perhaps you didn't ask her permission?'

'I appreciate the food and you listening, but I don't know what you're talking about. What would I need a cloak for? I have a uniform, at least, I used to.'

Charity gave a deep sigh.

'Tell me what you've been doing for the last couple of days.'

Isaac gave her an odd look but was sober enough to tell her, in some detail, about how busy all the servants had been packing up the house ready for Sir John and his family to leave and return to London.

'Everything had to be packed or moved,' he told her. 'There were two carriages for all their things to go back with them and then everything else was to be moved to one end of the house because his master is knocking down walls and putting up walls and the rooms all need to be empty. I've worked my boots off and what's the thanks I get?'

'And can anyone vouch for you?'

'What's that mean?' Isaac asked. 'Were you working on your own, or is there anyone who would swear what you've told me is true?'

'We were all working together, Tom, Joe, Little John and me. I couldn't have done it on my own.'

'Excellent,' Charity said, knowing she could prove Isaac was not the highwayman but then her heart sank because she doubted her sister could account for her movements in as much detail.

'And what about at night?' Charity continued. 'Do you have shared quarters? Are you ever on your own?'

'Joe and I share a room in the attic but only until the house is finished. Then I think we'll live above the barn. I don't much care for my own company. I suppose it would be different if I had a girl but none of us is courting.'

'Leave things with me,' Charity said. 'I'll do what I can for you and in the meantime if you speak to Whistler in the yard, he'll find you a bed for the night. Tell him I sent you.'

'Thanks, miss. I always said you were a good lass.'

⋆ ⋆ ⋆

The following few days were difficult for Charity. She was so tired she got some sleep but was woken by nightmares. Twice she found herself in a cold sweat dreaming of a noose around her neck and wondering how her father would manage the inn without her.

When she did manage to get up she was unsteady on her legs and her head ached so that it was impossible for her to think straight.

'What is wrong with you, lass?' her father asked as Charity stumbled and knocked over a wooden chair. 'I know you've not been drinking, but that's what it looks like to me.'

'Have you got a fever, miss?' Bessie asked as she picked up the overturned chair.

'I feel a bit flushed,' Charity admitted, 'but no fever and I swear not a drop has passed my lips.'

For a moment her eyes rested on her father and she wondered if she could

195

share her worst fears with him but it would be no good, she realised. However strong her evidence against Faith was, Peter Bell would never believe she would be capable of doing such a foolhardy thing.

'Go and lie down before you fall down,' her father told her. 'You're no use round here and if you have got a fever brewing, I don't want to catch it. Bessie will bring you up some broth later. Go and sleep it off, whatever it is.'

Charity had no energy to argue. Instead she turned and headed back to her straw mattress where she collapsed in a thankful heap and slept.

Sometime later Bessie brought her up a bowl of broth. Although Charity thanked her she didn't feel hungry but Bessie stood over her and made sure she at least had one sip.

'This is good, Bessie, thank you.' 'You look like a ghost, miss.'

Charity sat up and rubbed her head. For the first time she noticed a little posy of flowers beside her bed.

'That was a kind thought, Bessie, but I'm surprised you had time to pick flowers.'

'Those are from Moses, not me.'
'Moses?'

'He called by with some vegetables and asked where you were. Master said you were ill and on his way back he left those. I brought them up but you didn't even stir.'

Charity looked more closely at the posy of tiny pink rosebuds and knew where Moses had gone to get them.

Miss Rose had obviously told him how much she liked the pink roses and they had no smell so they were of no use to her in her rosewater making.

How kind, and how typical of Moses, to go to the trouble of choosing her favourite flowers to make her feel better! Perhaps he did care for her after all?

Charity remembered Moses had asked her to walk with him. Was that his way of suggesting they started to court? Why now of all times? Now she felt she wasn't worthy of him because of her dreadful secret and one that she could never share without betraying others.

'I might go down the lane for some air,' she told Bessie. 'Are you coping all right in the kitchen?'

'Master said we're only doing broth and bread and when it's gone, it's gone. The sun's shining, so most people will be out working in the fields until dusk. It might be busy then but we'll have a quiet day.'

Once Bessie had gone, Charity finished her soup and ran her fingers through her thick hair. Then she slowly and carefully headed for the brook with its icy cold water. That would wake her up even if nothing else did.

The fresh water felt good on her flushed cheeks and it got the sleep out of her eyes. She washed her face several times and scooped up the clear water to drink. It was the best she'd felt in days.

Without a backward glance, Charity headed into the field and down the little path that led away from the village. As a child, if she had ever been scolded by her mother, she could be found at the big tree.

The branches were such that it was easy to climb and, being summer it was now in full leaf so once she was in amongst the branches she was hidden from the world and could think. She felt she could be safe in the arms of the big oak tree.

The tree itself was huge but it wasn't very accessible. Bushes and leaves collected around its trunk and the path was so overgrown it was invisible to most. Charity fought her way to the trunk. The ground was a carpet of last year's acorns and many of them had sprouted into tiny saplings. She began to climb the tree.

Up in the branches she felt safe and secure and wished she could stay there for ever but knew she could only stay as long as it took for her to sort out a plan. She needed to think clearly and decide what must be done next.

She started to face the facts. The sad thing was, even in the clear light of day, all the evidence did still point towards

Faith. Her life was in danger, but only if Charity said anything and it was this burden that weighed heavily on her shoulders.

'I have to be sure,' Charity whispered to herself.

She thought back over the last few months and realised she had hardly seen anything of Faith. And worse still, when she did see Faith, her face and the scar was always concealed.

Charity reminisced about her childhood when she and her sisters had all hidden in the tree when they'd accidentally knocked over the bowl of peas they'd been shelling and when they'd eaten more blackberries than they should.

She couldn't help smiling at their happy childhood. They had been loved and free to roam and play. She thought of Joe and Whistler who were little more than children but they had to work long hours in the stables and doing jobs around the New Bell. Even Bessie did not have much time to be herself.

So wrapped up in her thoughts she

didn't hear the voices until they were practically underneath her. Two women were arguing. One had been crying and Charity could hear her sniffing and pleading.

Charity knew their voices and knew they too must have come to the sanctuary of the tree, just as she had done.

Hope screamed when she heard a movement in the tree above.

'Hush, it's only me.'

'Charity! What on earth are you doing up there?' Faith called.

'I'm probably here for the same reason as you.'

She jumped down and the three sisters hugged then squatted at the base of the trunk hidden from view by the thick vegetation all around them.

'I think I know the truth,' Charity began after a little while. 'I just don't understand why and I'm not sure what to do.'

'I told you she knows,' Hope hissed at her sister. 'And if Charity has worked it out, then others will. You're not safe and you have to do as I say.'

'What do you think you know?' Faith quietly asked her youngest sister. She sounded as cool as the icy brook, but it didn't fool Charity.

'I think you're the highwayman who held up Sir John and later the Dowager and someone else the other night.'

'And what makes you think that?' Faith asked, remaining calm as though they were discussing which material to choose for her next ball gown.

'Well, for a start you have that scar,' Charity pointed to her sister's cheek. The white arsenic powder she wore helped to cover it but all three girls knew it was there. Her lady's maid might also be suspicious and that was a worry.

'It was too much of a coincidence that the Dowager said she'd scratched her attacker and then you appeared with a scar on your face.'

'I have a kitten. Maybe the charming little cat scratched me?'

'Perhaps,' Charity conceded, 'but that is not all. On your wedding day you avoided me — you were covered in your veil and made a quick getaway so few people saw much of you.'

'We were sent away so we could ride in daylight with an armed guard. It was my father-in-law's wish that we should go early.'

'I went in your room. I found a signet ring.'

'You shouldn't have been snooping.'

Charity looked at her sister and had to hold back the tears.

'I missed you. I wanted to help you on your wedding day but you'd shut me out and I felt so hurt. I only wanted to touch something that was yours to feel close to you.'

Her words obviously had an impact on Faith.

'I did try and get you to come and join in with the dancing,' Hope reminded her sister.

'I didn't want to let you all down.'

The three of them sat in silence, all deep in their own thoughts.

'And then when we were at the

manor, I saw the receipt for a tri-cornered black hat made out in your name. That together with this latest attack and the coach driver cutting your cape told me without any doubt that you were involved.'

Again there was silence.

'So why?' Charity asked looking up into her sister's face. 'Why risk everything?'

'Some time ago I saw Matt the baker. He told me his eldest son was sick. He couldn't afford to pay for a doctor. I have no money of my own but I really wanted to help him.'

'But turning to crime?' Charity exclaimed, although she'd heard the child was very poorly.

'I can see now how reckless and foolish I was, but I only wanted to be able to help Matt. He'd saved my life and I've always felt in his debt.'

'But you haven't sold Sir John's signet ring,' Charity said.

'I'm ashamed to say I did sell the jewellery he'd bought for his wife. I paid a doctor to treat the sick child and he's recovering well.'

'So why not leave it there?' Charity asked.

'I wish I had! The truth was, it was exciting, and it felt good to help others. I can't believe how silly I've been.'

Up until now Hope had been listening but not saying a great deal. She was now playing with a blade of grass, winding it round her finger and then smoothing it out.

'I do know how Faith feels,' she said at last. 'And I could have done the same.'

Her sisters both looked at her in surprise because out of the three of them, Hope had been the most ladylike and more like their mother. 'That was until I met Rev Mason and fell in love with him.'

'Oh gosh!' Faith said. 'Please marry him in haste because if I am caught and tried he may disown you.'

'I cannot guarantee that he would understand the situation, but I know he does love me and he would pray for your soul.'

Charity was beginning to feel sorry for her sister. She was glad they'd had a chance to talk and for her to explain so that now she could start to understand.

'But what you did was wrong,' Charity said quietly.

'I know, but no-one was hurt, and my intentions were good.'

'A great many people could have been affected by your behaviour if Sir John had decided not to move to Twyford. The vast majority of the village rely on him for work. Some would starve without it.'

'I didn't think about that. I didn't even know it was Sir John until one of the maids was talking about it later.'

Charity so wanted to forgive her sister but this was a serious offence and Charity had made a promise to Sir John in front of witnesses and formed an allegiance with Constable Hargreaves.

She was in an impossible situation and she didn't think Faith was aware of it.

'This is my problem,' Charity told

Faith and explained her dilemma.

'You could be a real heroine if you arrested me now and marched me to the gallows!'

'Faith! That's an awful thing to say,' Hope told her.

'But it's true.' Faith lowered her head. 'I have been silly and foolish and I shall have to make amends.'

'But how?' Hope asked.

'James is a generous husband. I have already asked him for a small sum with which to help others. I intend to buy back the jewellery and return it and the signet ring along with everything else I've taken. I solemnly promise never to be so reckless again.'

'We ought to go or we'll be missed and then we'll have more explaining to do,' Hope said with her voice of reason.

The girls hugged each other tightly. No more was said between them but Charity felt the closeness and unity they'd once had was back now they'd shared an open and honest conversation.

On her way home Charity realised she

was no longer suffering with an aching head.

Talking with her sisters had lightened her load. It was a good feeling to know that the strong bond she shared with them had returned and together they would be strong, no matter what happened.

As Charity approached the New Bell she had an idea. Once inside she quietly got on with her work, making sure to thank Bessie for her extra help.

It was inevitable that sooner or later she would come across a group of men discussing the latest highwaymen attack. Charity had her plan ready and was quick to remind them of the false claims recently made about being held up by highwaymen and perhaps this was just another tale. She told them of Thomas Chandler's story and how he nearly got away with 1,000 pounds.

Charity noticed Isaac the footman who had spent the morning with the lads in the stables grooming the horses in order to pay for his keep. She wasn't the only one who had seen him, Bessie had hardly taken her eyes off him. Charity smiled in his direction and knew she had to clear his name.

Just as they were clearing up and about to close the inn, Luke appeared.

'Is Moses here?'

'He's over there in the corner,' Peter said. 'You'll have to be quick — he looks as though he's about to leave.'

Charity looked up. She'd been so deep in thought she'd not even noticed him. She looked in his direction now but he just scowled at her.

'I have a special letter for you,' Luke said to Moses, holding the letter in one hand and his hand out for a penny with his other.

'I have no money to pay you and no wish to receive this letter,' Moses told him.

'It's not from Molly, if that what's troubling you,' Luke whispered but Charity was standing close enough to hear.

'I've got work to do,' Moses said and headed for the door.

'What's up with him?' Luke asked but everyone else was watching Moses leave. It was certainly so out of character. Moses was usually such a friendly, happy person who would always take a few minutes to talk. Perhaps the episode with Molly had really shaken him more than Charity realised.

That's another thing I must do, she told herself. I have to clear Isaac's name and thank Moses for the flowers.

She thought back to what Hope said about being in love and what a wonderful feeling that was. Charity just felt a stab of pain when Moses had glared at her and then had left without a backward glance let alone a cheery wave.

Luke was sitting at the bar chatting with Mr Bell.

'I don't know what to do with this letter now,' he was saying. 'I suppose I shall have to return it to the sender.'

'He seemed a bit out of sorts just now. Why not hold on to it and try to deliver it again when he's in a better frame of mind?'

'I would but what if the letter needs an urgent reply?' Luke argued.

Peter Bell looked at Charity then reached for the pot where he kept their money. He took out a penny and handed it to Luke.

'I'll see he gets it.'

Luke hesitated. He and Samuel knew they were only to hand over information to the recipient and not ever to any third party, but Luke was a bright boy and realised he could trust Mr Bell the landlord.

'Don't ever say I've done this, or I'll lose my job.'

One Good Deed

Before Luke left the inn, Charity pulled him aside.

'I have a message for you to take to my sister Hope.'

'It'll cost you,' he said. 'You know the going rate.'

'I do,' Charity told him holding out a coin. 'You're to tell Hope discreetly that she is to reinstate Isaac.'

'Is that it?' Luke asked as he stood waiting for the rest of the message.

'That's enough,' Charity told him. 'She will understand. I won't need a reply. And you don't need to tell anyone else about this, understood?'

'Understood,' Luke confirmed.

That following day was warm and the farm labourers were able to work late but once the sun set they headed for the ale houses and a well-earned pint.

'Have you seen Moses tonight?' Charity asked her father but he shook his head.

The letter for him was still sitting in the kitchen.

Samuel arrived and entered the New Bell as though he were the town crier. He drank a pint of ale in one and clearly enjoyed the looks he was getting. Everyone could tell he had important news to share.

'I delivered an important letter today,' Samuel announced, clearing his throat, 'and I have been given permission to disclose its contents. Indeed, I have been paid handsomely to pass this on.

'Sir John has received a letter from the very highwayman who attacked him . . . ' There were jeers and cheers. It was obvious that not everyone believed Samuel's story or that the letter from the alleged culprit was genuine.

'It's up to you whether you believe me or not but the letter told Sir John where he could find his signet ring and his box of jewels for his wife and daughters and sure enough when he went to look, there they all were with a written apology and a promise that he had reformed his wicked ways.'

There was stunned silence in the bar as the men took in this unlikely story.

'I think that calls for a celebration,' Charity said loudly, glancing at her father because if all the men drank just one more pint each, it would increase their takings considerably.

Fortunately the men cheered and began to order more jugs of ale.

Luke arrived with a message for Isaac. He was now making himself useful rolling in a fresh barrel of beer.

'I have a message for you, sir,' Luke announced looking straight at Isaac, 'and have no fear the duty has already been paid.

'You can have your old job back as footman. There was a misunderstanding and you have to report for work in the morning with no hard feelings.'

'Sir John must be so pleased to have his possessions back that he's pardoning everyone.' Someone laughed.

'Luke didn't say he'd been pardoned, he said he was never guilty in the first

place. He said there was a misunderstanding, there's a difference.'

'Sorry, Miss Charity, I'm not as clever
with words as you.'

'And I didn't mean to sound so cross,'
Charity replied. 'The important thing is
that Sir John and his family are here to
stay and Isaac has his job back.'

'I'll drink to that,' the man said.

'You got your way, then,' Moses said
to Charity. 'Your man got his job back.'

'My man?' Charity repeated. 'What
do you mean?'

'I saw you the other night sitting at his
table listening to his story. You only had
eyes for him and I wouldn't be surprised
if your sisters had a hand in making sure
Sir John pardoned him.'

Charity bristled at his words.

'Isaac was wrongly accused and now
it's been sorted. There is nothing more
to be said about it and I am surprised at
you for not wanting justice to be done.'

'So long as you're happy,' Moses said
with a twisted grin.

'What's got into you?' Charity said

looking up into the familiar face. 'You hardly acknowledged me earlier and now you're treating me as though I've done something wrong.

'Oh my ... Moses! I didn't thank you for the flowers. Such a lot has happened, it slipped my mind. Thank you, it was a lovely thought.'

Charity stood on her tiptoes about to give Moses a sisterly peck on the cheek for his kindness but Moses stepped away.

'I bet Isaac didn't pick your favourite flowers.'

Charity froze on the spot taken aback by Moses moving away from her as well as being confused by Moses's attitude to Isaac.

'Are you jealous?' she asked in disbelief but before he had the opportunity to answer, Mr Bell thrust the letter into his hand.

'You might want to read it in the kitchen.

There's a lot of prying eyes in here.'

Moses slipped the letter into his jacket

unopened, nodded to Mr Bell and left. However, a moment later he returned and silently popped a penny on the bar in front of Peter Bell, nodded and left as quietly as he'd arrived.

Charity followed him out but Moses kept on walking away back towards his farm.

She stood and watched him, wondering why he would be jealous. She had only wanted to make sure justice was done. She had no romantic feelings toward Isaac and even if she had, it was of no concern of anyone's.

Suddenly she felt a large hand on her shoulder, making her jump.

Charity gave a little scream but as she turned round to see James her brother-in- law she gasped instead.

'James! Is everything all right with Faith?' Charity's heart started to beat rapidly fearing Faith was in danger despite her efforts to put things right.

'Faith is well,' he told her. 'It is you I wanted to see. In fact Faith suggested you might be the person to help me.'

'What is it you want?' Charity asked, feeling a little suspicious of her brother-in- law. He may be married to her sister but she didn't really know him.

'I know you can be discreet. I wouldn't want everyone to know, but I am extremely fond of your sister but unfortunately I have to travel more often than I would wish now I am a married man.

'I wish to have a portrait painted of Faith. I just require a small one, a miniature that I can keep about my person and take with me when I travel. Faith said I was to speak with you.'

Charity led James into the kitchen. She sat him down with a bowl of broth and searched in the drawer in the dresser for Joe's sketch of the stranger who came into the inn when her father had been away.

'I know it's only a charcoal sketch, but I can assure you it is a true likeness. I'm sure if Joe had proper training or the use of paints, he would do his best to capture Faith's image.'

James studied the sketch. Charity looked over his shoulder and realised that perhaps it was very simple and bore no resemblance to the fine paintings she'd seen on the walls at the manor and the other fine houses she'd visited.

'I like this. It has a natural charm about it that reminds me of Faith. Between you and me, I sometimes wonder if she is happy being a fine lady.'

'Of course she's happy,' Charity said rather too quickly. 'I know she is, although have you thought she might like to travel with you?'

'I would like to meet this artist. Can you arrange that?'

'Wait here,' Charity told him as she went to find Joe.

Before the evening was over Joe had his first commission. James had given him money for paper and finer quality charcoal. It was agreed Joe would do a series of sketches of Faith, all small enough to fit in her husband's pocket so he could take them away with him. Bessie thought it was the most romantic gesture she had ever heard and even Charity had to give James credit for his actions.

* * *

Peter Bell announced over breakfast that he was going over to spend a day with Miss Rose helping her with several of the jobs she needed doing and to see how the new ladies were getting on harvesting the rose petals and learning how to make rose water the way Miss Rose wanted it to be done.

'Shall I make you some food to take with you?' Charity asked as she rolled up her sleeves, ready to work.

'There's no need. Miss Rose will make sure I am well looked after.'

Charity looked at her father. He was practically back to his old self these days but she still worried about him.

'Are you going to walk to Hurst?' she asked.

'Big Tom was telling me there is a coach due to pass through the village this morning and it will travel through

Hurst, so I am hoping to catch a lift. He said he'd send over one of his boys when the coach arrives.'

Charity was surprised her father had got himself so organised but as far as she was concerned it was good news. He was feeling fit and healthy again and pleased to be able to help others by fixing things, which was always what he did best.

Later that morning, a boy arrived to tell her father that the coach had arrived. Mr Bell kissed Charity goodbye and disappeared with a skip in his step.

Charity noticed a difference in Bessie. She'd started to take more care of herself. She combed her hair and tried hard to keep her apron clean.

'So who is the man in your life?' she asked but Bessie refused to say a word. Charity was pleased for her but at the same time she felt protective and didn't want the girl hurt or messed about.

She soon realised she had nothing to worry about when Isaac appeared.

At first she thought nothing of it because he came round the back to speak to Joe and Whistler who'd befriended him when he thought he'd lost his job.

Half an hour later she was surprised to find Isaac sitting in the kitchen chatting with Bessie.

Charity was about to scold him for stopping her working when she realised this was the man Bessie was so keen on. She bit her tongue and decided to see how things were going to develop.

Bessie had little experience of flirting. She suddenly became very shy but Isaac was obviously smitten, too, and made sure he kept her talking while she worked away at her chores.

'And how are things up at the manor?' Charity asked. 'Have you seen anything of my sisters?'

'I hear they are planning to visit again soon to see what has been done with the place. Lady Mary is keen to move in properly.'

'Is the manor habitable now?' Charity asked.

'There is a lot to be done, in my opinion, but you would notice a difference.

Sir John misses his wife and family when they're not there, so he encourages them to visit.'

'That's good. Maybe I shall see Faith and Hope when they are next here,' Charity said and thought again of having to dress up in her pale blue gown, hoping that Lady Mary would not realise it was the same dress she had worn the last time they'd met.

'Miss Faith has been away visiting her husband's family. They hadn't been back since their wedding.'

Charity nodded as she recalled her sister's wedding and how she had not really enjoyed her time away.

'Did you realise the Dowager was held up by highwaymen around the time of the wedding?' Isaac asked.

'I think I did hear something about that,' Charity said vaguely as she tried to look very busy in the kitchen. 'It hasn't happened again, has it?'

'Oh, no,' Isaac told her, 'quite the opposite. The highwaymen had taken her jewels but mysteriously these have now been returned with an apology. The Dowager was most surprised, saying she hadn't expected to ever see her pearls again.' Charity smiled.

'That's very good news.'

'It must have been the same highway-man who took Sir John's things because he has had his jewels returned with a note.'

'Perhaps he had one of Bessie's dreams which made him see the error of his ways,' Charity said, trying to bring her back into the conversation. 'Perhaps you and Bessie could go and fetch some water from the well?'

Charity watched as Isaac insisted on carrying both the buckets.

As the sun was beginning to set a tired Peter Bell arrived back at the inn.

'And how was Miss Rose?' Charity asked. 'Miss Rose is well but it hasn't really worked out with Miss Baldwin and the other lasses who were supposed to help her.

'All they seem to want to do is to chatter away and, to be honest, it is a long way for them to go. Miss Baldwin has been offered an apprenticeship with Mrs Brown the milliner and she's delighted about that.

'Another of the girls is betrothed and will be helping on her husband's farm, so I don't think the yield of rose water will be very high this year. To be honest, it's easy for the girls to get jobs in the village now rather than travelling over to Hurst.'

A Mystery Aunt

The very next day Faith arrived in her carriage. She looked more comfortable in a simple dress rather than the finery she often wore nowadays.

Joe sat her down on a chair in the yard and sketched her from every angle. All his pictures were serious but then Whistler made her laugh with his witty tune and Joe stopped. 'I must do one more.'

'Another one?' Faith groaned. 'I've been sitting here for ever and I'm stiff. I fear I shall turn into a statue if I have to stay still much longer.'

'No problem, just talk to Whistler and pretend I'm not here.'

Faith laughed and let out a sigh of relief. 'I had no idea sitting for a portrait, especially a tiny one, could be so exhausting.'

'Let me entertain you,' Whistler offered and immediately began to whistle one of his tunes.

Instantly Charity could see Faith relax as she tapped her feet to the familiar tune, and clap her hands. As he came to the chorus she joined in.

Her voice was sweet and tuneful and together they made an entertaining pair.

Charity smiled. She didn't feel she'd been blessed with a pretty voice. She'd always admired the way Faith could mimic other people and the way she could sing.

Sometimes in church she would start the first verse of a hymn as quiet and timid as the church cat and then during the refrain she'd belt out the words with great gusto along with everyone else, and then finally she'd sing the last verse sweetly with such confidence and clarity it was a pleasure to listen to.

Looking at her now, Charity could see how easily she'd have found it to mimic a man's voice when she impersonated a highwayman and no-one would have been any the wiser.

Sincerely Charity hoped she'd learned from the experience and from now on would use her obvious talents in a much more positive way and entertain others as she was doing now.

They all clapped once the song ended but immediately Whistler started up another tune, one everyone was sure to know. Even Bessie had set aside her broom and was clapping along.

It was good, Charity thought, to see her happier in herself these days. She responded well to being treated kindly and praised for the things she did well and encouraged with the chores she struggled with.

Bessie was happier too because Isaac had become a frequent visitor when he was in the area and the two of them had become firm friends.

Charity watched for a little while longer but then felt herself being observed. She looked up and saw Moses standing by the wall. When he noticed he'd been spotted he approached her. She had no idea how long he'd been standing there.

'I'm sure you are busy but could you spare me a few minutes to walk with me?

I have something important to show you. It won't take long.'

Charity looked him up and down. Moses was wearing what looked like his Sunday best, even though it wasn't Sunday and he should have been working on the farm.

Perhaps he'd come to apologise for his strange behaviour?

They walked along the high street to the meandering brook, over the little bridge and into the field following the path Charity had taken recently when she'd headed for the big oak tree.

'Read this,' Moses said and showed Charity the letter he'd recently received which had so nearly been returned to its sender.

Moses had been an orphan abandoned as a baby for Mr and Mrs Lamb to find and to bring up as their own. Mr Polehampton, a local man made good, died a bachelor leaving money for ten poor boys to be taught to read and write and for a school, chapel and dwelling house to be built.

Moses benefited from his generosity and had passed on his knowledge to his eager friend Charity Bell who, being a girl, did not qualify for Twyford Boys School.

Both Moses and Charity had been keen to learn. Neither Faith nor Hope had shown much interest but had learned the basics from their mother.

The letter was from Moses's great-aunt Faithful's solicitor. It transpired that she had recently died and left him a modest but handsome sum, but only if he married a local girl. Charity instinctively knew Faith had something to do with this.

'The thing is,' Moses said with a frown on his face, 'I was left in a Moses basket and no-one ever knew who I belonged to. I'm sure this must be some mistake.'

'Perhaps this great aunt went to the trouble of tracking you down.'

'That's what the solicitor said, too.'

'So you've been to see him already?'

'I thought it was some sort of trick but it is genuine and that's why I'm here.'

Moses took Charity's hand in his and knelt down on one knee. 'Charity, would you do me the honour of being my wife?'

What Does the Future Hold?

Charity gasped. When the sun woke her up that morning little did she realise that this would be the day that Moses proposed and that she refused …

'Moses, I can't marry you,' she said sadly and tried to withdraw her hand. 'Hope made me realise the other day that I must only marry for love and you love me only as a sister.'

Moses began to interrupt but Charity continued.

'I know it is possible for people to grow to love each other in time, as Faith and James have done, but … '

'But Charity — I have always loved you and please don't think I'm only asking you now because I want this inheritance.

'You can ask your father because he knows I asked for your hand long ago and he had granted it, but he told me I had to let you be yourself before you became my wife.

'That's why I tried to help you become the constable's assistant and landlady of the New Bell. I wonder now if you will be satisfied to be simply my wife?'

'But do you love me?' Charity asked, turning her head away from him so he wouldn't see the pain in her face.

'I am not good with words like this, but I do know I never walk the short cut to the ford but always take the long route round in the hope of catching a glimpse of you.'

'Really?'

'Really,' Moses told her. 'And one of the first things I intend to do is to commission Joe to make a sketch of you, for me to carry near to my heart so I can see you whenever I want to.' Moses rose to his feet and brushed himself down.

'You don't need to say anything now. I will show you how much I am in love with you and hopefully that will make you feel the same about me and then together we can go and see the preacher.'

'But I do love you,' Charity told him,

throwing her arms around him. 'I dream of you. My heart misses a beat when I see you and I knew that only you would go to the trouble of picking my favourite flowers.'

Moses cupped his hand gently around Charity's chin and drew her into a warm kiss. Charity had never been kissed before. Moses's lips were soft.

'Shall we go and tell everyone the good news?' he asked. 'With any luck Faith will still be having her portrait done and you can tell her.'

'I haven't even said yes.' Charity laughed. 'But you kissed me, so now you'll have to marry me.' Eagerly Moses told her of the plans he had.

'I am fortunate to have a farm. I'd like to use this money to help people just as Mr and Mrs Lamb helped me when I was an abandoned baby.'

'Oh, Moses, that's such a wonderful thing to do. I shall do all I can to help, too.'

The two of them skipped back to the New Bell but no-one took any notice of them.

There was a crowd of people around Faith, who had collapsed.

'Get back,' Bessie shouted. 'She needs some air.'

'What's wrong?' Charity asked, rushing to her side. 'Are you ill?'

'Not ill exactly,' Faith said. 'You see, I am with child and sometimes I come over a little light-headed.'

The two sisters hugged and shared their news. Faith's carriage was sent to fetch Hope to join them for the rest of the day so the three of them could be together.

Just as Hope arrived, so did Constable Hargreaves. Charity's heart sank as he looked from her to Faith and back again. Hope drew closer and took Faith's hand. The three of them stood united.

The air was so thick with tension that you could almost taste it. It was like a storm brewing.

Faith looked ashen. She was trembling. Hope held her one side and Charity the other. Carefully they eased her back into the chair while Bessie fetched her some water.

Moses broke the mood by walking up to the constable and offering his hand.

'My apologies, sir,' he said. 'I know you are like a second father to Charity and I realise now I should have asked you for your permission before I proposed to her.'

'You've proposed at last?' Constable Hargreaves gave a rare smile and patted Moses on the back.

'I hope she said yes, although that could mean I need to be looking for another assistant.'

'I am happy to carry on,' Charity reassured him, 'at least for the time being,' she added as she came to stand beside Moses.

'Good,' Hargreaves said, 'I need you to come with me. We have an important matter to discuss and the sooner the better.'

Charity looked back at her sisters. Faith did not look well and probably needed to take a nap. Hope gave her a little nod.

Charity looked at Moses.

'Do you need me?' he asked.

'No, just your good lady. Come along, we mustn't keep Sir John waiting.'

'Sir John?'

'Yes. I believe you made him a promise? I know nothing more except that's what he wants to discuss and he asked me to be there as a witness.'

'A witness?'

'Must you repeat everything I say?'

Charity's stomach lurched as she hurried along beside Constable Hargreaves.

At the crossroads they turned right and came to a stop outside the chapel. Sir John was waiting, deep in conversation with the minister.

Charity's mouth felt dry but the palms of her hands were damp. Was she going to be questioned in front of Constable Hargreaves who did his very best to keep law and order in the town?

And was the minister there so she would have to swear the truth before God? How had Faith managed to get

her into this mess? Would they understand why she had put her family first
now that Faith had done what she could
to set things right?

'Good morning, Miss Bell.' Sir John
greeted her with a friendly smile.

Charity was too anxious to smile back.
In fact she was instantly suspicious and
guessed he was only trying to make her
relax and fall into his trap.

'I don't know if you are aware of the
fact that I recently received a letter from
the vagabond who robbed me. He swore
he was sorry and told me where I would
find my property.

'It has now been safely recovered and
the culprit, although his name is still a
mystery, has promised to make amends.'

The whole of Twyford had heard of
this letter that Sir John had received and
everyone knew he had had his signet ring
and jewels returned.

'I did hear of your good news,' Charity said cautiously. She prayed he would
now let the matter be forgotten.

'Miss Bell, you, out of all the people

of Berkshire were brave enough to stand up to me and make me consider my actions. I admit I had not given it sufficient thought as to what would happen if I moved elsewhere leaving the manor empty again.'

Charity nodded. She could feel her cheeks burning and her heart pounding.

'Although the thief has not been found and convicted, the constable and I believe he is little more than a petty criminal and has seen the error of his ways. In fact now he's put things right here, he's probably moved on and we shall never see nor hear of him again.'

'That's good,' Charity whispered with a huge sigh. 'The matter is now closed then,' she added and stole a tentative look at Constable Hargreaves. She couldn't tell if he suspected anything was amiss.

'I am indebted to you, Miss Bell,' Sir John told her. 'In fact I think the whole of Twyford ought to thank you for your courage and determination. I wish to reward you in some way.'

'There is no need,' Charity's cheeks

were still flushed and she had been looking down at her feet feeling ashamed that she was being praised when she had concealed the true identity of the culprit. She raised her eyes to look at Sir John.

'All I wish is for you and your family to remain in the area and to use the local people for all your needs so that the village benefits.'

'I am happy to do that and have already instructed my wife and my household to shop for their produce locally, although of course there are certain items we have to send to London for.'

Charity nodded although she had no idea what you could possibly get in London that you couldn't get in Twyford.

'I would like to do something for you,' he continued. 'I could commission a statue . . . ' Charity laughed and Hargreaves looked a little shocked at the idea. 'But I suspect you would prefer something more practical?'

'Thank you, Sir John,' Charity began. 'I am shortly going to marry Moses Lamb.' She glanced at the minister. 'We are coming to see you very soon, sir, I promise, but everything's happened so quickly.

'Moses was an orphan and he has a small sum from an aunt. Together we want to help people when they fall on hard times - maybe if a child was ill and needed a doctor, for example. Perhaps you can help us with this?'

'Consider it done. Once you and Mr Lamb are wed, come and tell me what you need.'

'Thank you, sir. We will indeed.'

★ ★ ★

Six months had gone by.

'I can't believe you're really going,' Charity said as she looked at Hope and at the large array of travelling trunks surrounding her.

'I'm not sure I can believe it either, but this time next week Rev Mason and I shall be on the ship taking us on our adventure.'

Rev Mason, it turned out, was a kindred spirit. He too longed for a more exciting life than being rector of a small chapel and so had applied to become a missionary and to take God's word to the far corners of the earth.

Now the time had come for he and Hope to say their goodbyes and set sail.

'I am so glad I was able to meet my little nephew,' Hope said. 'I wonder how much little James John will have grown by the time I see him again?'

There was a silence in the air as they all wondered if Hope would ever see any of them again.

Travelling on the sea to foreign parts was fraught with dangers but now was not a time to dwell on what could go wrong but on how fortunate they all were.

James bent down to admire his son and once again to congratulate Faith on how clever she was to produce such a perfect child for him. He seemed quite besotted with the two of them.

Charity was pleased to see how fondly they looked at each other these days. She was delighted too that they had bought a small manor house only a few miles away and that she and Faith could continue to see each other regularly.

'We shall have to come to an arrangement with Samuel and Luke so that we can share news between our households,' Charity suggested to Faith, 'just as Miss Rose and her sisters do.'

Moses, James and Rev Mason went to study the maps of where the ship would take them.

'Do you still crave adventure?' Hope asked Faith quietly.

'I am starting a new adventure of my own,' Faith told her as she hugged her new baby. 'I have such hopes for my son and pray we shall be blessed with more children. You won't believe it but I feel so differently now I have a child to protect.'

'And you, Charity?' Hope asked. 'What adventures lie in store for you?'

'Moses and I are going to provide food and accommodation for wee waifs and teach the men how to farm so that they will be able to fend for themselves and the girls will learn to help Miss Rose harvest the petals and make rosewater to sell in the village.'

Charity was pleased that her father was now completely recovered. Joe, Whistler and Bessie remained at the New Bell and continued to help him with the running of the inn.

Isaac and Bessie had started courting and Miss Rose had been to visit the New Bell — not that she had any interest in sampling the ale. Her only interest seemed to be in Peter Bell, the landlord.

'I always knew you would marry Moses,'

Hope told her, 'even when you were both eight or nine years old.'

Charity stroked her belly, feeling the new life growing inside her and knew she, too, was starting a new adventure — alongside her dear Moses.

We do hope that you have enjoyed reading this large print book.

Did you know that all of our titles are available for purchase?

We publish a wide range of high quality large print books including:
Romances, Mysteries, Classics
General Fiction
Non Fiction and Westerns

Special interest titles available in large print are:
The Little Oxford Dictionary
Music Book, Song Book
Hymn Book, Service Book

Also available from us courtesy of Oxford University Press:
Young Readers' Dictionary
(large print edition)
Young Readers' Thesaurus
(large print edition)

For further information or a free brochure, please contact us at:
Ulverscroft Large Print Books Ltd.,
The Green, Bradgate Road, Anstey,
Leicester, LE7 7FU, England.
Tel: (00 44) 0116 236 4325
Fax: (00 44) 0116 234 0205

Other titles in the
Linford Romance Library:

PROMISE OF SPRING

Beth Francis

After the breakdown of her relation-
ship with Justin, Amy moves out of
town to a small village. In her cosy
cottage, with her kind next-door
neighbour Meg, she's determined
to make a fresh start. But there are
complications in store. Though Amy
has sworn never to risk her heart
again, she finds her friendship with
Meg's great-nephew Mike deepening
into something more. Until Mike's
ex-girlfriend Emma reappears on the
scene — and so does Justin ...

DATE WITH DANGER

Jill Barry

Bonnie spends carefree summers in the Welsh seaside resort where her mother runs a guesthouse. But things will change after she meets Patrik, a young Hungarian funfair worker. Both she and her friend Kay find love in the heady whirl of the fair – and are also are fast learning how people they thought they knew can sometimes conceal secrets. As Patrik moonlights for one of her mother's friends, Bonnie fears that he may be heading into danger ...

ROSE'S ALPINE ADVENTURE

Christina Garbutt

Rose is in need of excitement. Taking a leap of faith, she flies to the Alps to take up the position of personal assistant to Olympic ski champion Liam Woods. Though she's never skied before — or even spent much time around snow — that's not going to stop her! But she hadn't bargained on someone trying to sabotage Liam's new venture ... or on her attraction to him. Can she and Liam save his business — and will he fall for her too?

A BODY IN THE CHAPEL

Philippa Carey

Ipswich, 1919: On her way to teach Sunday School, Margaret Preston finds a badly injured man unconscious at the chapel gate. She and her widowed father, Reverend Preston, take him in and call the doctor. When the stranger regains consciousness, he tells them he has lost his memory, not knowing who he is or how he came to be there. As he and Margaret grow closer, their fondness for one another increases. But she is already being courted by another man …

BLETCHLEY SECRETS

Dawn Knox

1940: A cold upbringing with parents who unfairly blame her for a family tragedy has robbed Jess of all self-worth and confidence. Escaping to join the WAAF, she's stationed at RAF Holsmere, until a seemingly unimportant competition leads to her recruitment into the secret world of code-breaking at Bletchley Park. Love, however, eludes her: the men she chooses are totally unsuitable — until she meets Daniel. But there is so much which separates them. Can they ever find happiness together?